I Deserve

Alicia J. Evans

Copyright © 2022 Alicia Evans

Wind Beneath My Wings Publishing

Editing by Tamykah Anthony (Busy Bee Publications)

ISBN: 979-8-9852349-1-6

Dedication

This book is dedicated to my parents
Leroy & Jural Evans, and my siblings Reecie, Bunnie & Anthony.

Acknowledgments

I must first thank God, for blessing me with the desire
to entertain and the passion for spinning a tale.

I must also thank my older brother Michael "Mike" Evans for
inspiring my love for reading. This ignited my passion for writing.

Next, I want to thank my other half, Nathaniel
Croskey. Your love, patience, and support in
everything I do means the world to me.

To my baby brother Leroy "Doc" Evans, thank you for reading
the very first draft and encouraging me to continue.

To my wonderful Sisters of Sugar & Spice Book Club: Tatia,
Tawanna, Gail, Annye, Suzie, Cathy, Dannielle, Asha.
Your love and encouragement on this journey could not be
summed up in words. For you all to keep asking me "what's
up with the book?" or to tell me "I'm still waiting" has been
the force I needed to complete this work, and I thank you.

Thank you Gayla E. Leath for editing the first draft and letting me know *nicely* I had work to do. I am grateful for your honesty.

I would be remiss if I did not give a huge Thank you to Tamykah Anthony. Thank You for all you have done to assist with getting my first *book baby* out into the world. Your editing and your words of encouragement throughout the whole process kept me motivated.

To all of you that showed me any support, I thank you. And finally, to you, the readers, *thank you*. You could have picked up any book, but you chose ***I Deserve*** and for that I am eternally grateful.

Alrighty then enjoy the ride!!!!!
Ciao!

Love is patient, love is kind. It does not envy, it does not boast, it is not proud. It does not dishonor others, it is not self-seeking, it is not easily angered, it keeps no record of wrongs.
1 Corinthians 13: 4-5

"It's going to be a good day…it's going to be a good day," I tell myself repeatedly, allowing it to become my mantra for the day. I close my eyes and say a silent prayer for strength as I reflect on what just happened. Yes, strength is exactly what I know I will need this Friday morning after being awakened by an early morning call from Jeffery, my divorce lawyer.

"Hello" I say, still somewhere in that liminal space between being asleep and awake.

"Good morning, Alexia, sorry to call so early but I received a message from David's lawyer last night."

Jeffery's law firm handled my parents' estate for years. When I was searching for a lawyer, he was the only one I considered for my divorce. His work hours are not your typical 9am to 5pm, but they are perfect for me. With owning a small law firm, he is usually in the office late at night and then back again early in the morning. He spends the remainder of his day in court or meeting with clients.

As I roll over and glance at the digital clock on the nightstand, the glowing block numbers read 5:00am. What Jeffery says is enough to fully wake me up on the wrong side of the bed.

In a split second, I'm thinking, "I can't take any more of this. I really need this to be over. What more can David do to me?" Instinctively, I look above my bed at my favorite painting; it's supposed to be an abstract piece, but all I see is a Black woman exuding unlimited strength and power that I sometimes find myself tapping into.

My heartbeat quickens. The headache that had once been a constant nag while I was dealing with David, is now starting to creep back.

"Jeffery what has happened now?" I ask as I try to get my bearings together in the darkness of the early morning. The vibrant teal walls of my bedroom are shrouded in blackness without the sunlight.

"David has decided not to fight you anymore on the divorce." I heard Jeffery saying the words, but my grogginess and utter disbelief delayed my understanding of what I was hearing.

"What?!" I scream out as I kick the covers off and swing my feet to the floor, now sitting on the edge of the bed. I must have lost my bonnet getting up as I can now feel my honey-blonde locs tickling the middle of my back. With my free hand, I fumble in the dark to turn on the bedside lamp, hoping the extra light would help the words sink in.

"Jeffery, why now? After all this time?" I ask, now fully awake. "He has been fighting me since I first filed. I cannot believe he just decided to have a good heart."

"Alexia, call my office after nine o'clock this morning and speak with Tracey. She will give you an appointment for this evening. We can talk then, and I can give you all the details," Jeffery says reassuringly. "Alexia, this is good news. Whatever the reason, you should be happy. It will finally be over," he adds before disconnecting the call.

I sit listening to the dead silence on the other end for what feels like an eternity before my brain could send the signal to my arm to put the phone down. On the surface, I am elated that I can now almost taste my freedom, but I cannot help feeling a little suspicious and confused. After 2 years of contesting the divorce, he is finally giving in. My thoughts are so occupied that only muscle memory can account for how I am able to shower and get ready for the day.

David and I started having issues when he realized that I could make it without him. He was under the misguided notion that without him, I would fail. I proved him wrong. I opened the doors to my dream, *Chocolate, Books & More Café*. Owning my own café had been a dream of mine since before David came into my life. And now it is my reality.

I will never forget when I came up with the idea for a café. It was a cold snowy New York night in December with temperatures in the low 20's. I was at the bus stop on Hillside Avenue and 179th street in Queens, waiting on the bus that would take me home. The commute from LaGuardia Community College, where I was attending evening classes, was usually an hour. That night, however, it was much longer. It took an hour for the #7 train to even arrive. The F train was in the station when we needed to transfer, but it just creeped all the way to the last stop, 179th Street Hillside Avenue. With the wind blowing around me and snow falling at a quick steady pace, I remember feeling like I was literally freezing. Even with my puffy down coat, hat and gloves, I was not protected against the bitter cold. Glancing down Hillside Avenue in the direction of the bus, all I could see was darkness and the headlights of an occasional car passing by. There weren't any establishments open that I could use for shelter. Even Burger King, which was a staple in the area, was closed. That is the moment *it* came to me: the idea to own a coffee shop/bookstore near a bus stop or bus terminal. A place where customers could warm their hands while sipping on a hot beverage paired with a sweet treat AND pick up a book or a magazine while they wait on their bus. Everyone that has ever lived in New York knows how unreliable the New York City Transit buses and trains can be. There is no good reason a person should be out in the cold or the smoldering heat while waiting on public transportation. That night I started putting together a business plan.

I met David my sophomore year at LaGuardia Community College. He was a Finance major and I was a Business major. He was walking eye candy and I developed a sweet tooth for him. At six feet three inches tall and a solid 220lbs, David walked with a confidence that commanded the attention of everyone around. I immediately thought we would be great together. We complimented each other well; physically, his sandy brown complexion to my mocha latte hue, his clean-cut fade to my honey blond shoulder length locs. Whenever we entered a room together, people would stop and stare. I may not have had an hourglass figure but my 5 foot 4 inches 195lbs frame was stacked just right.

When I first met him, I thought he was my very own prince charming. He did not miss a beat when it came to opening doors and pulling out chairs for me, he constantly reminded me of how beautiful I was and was extremely protective of me. He reminded me a little of my dad in that way and my parents had been married half a century, so I just knew that I hit the jackpot with this Black man. We dated for a year before we got engaged and then we were married six months later.

I did not share my dream about the bookstore with him during the entire time we dated. Maybe in the back of my mind I knew he would not like it. Although David had some amazing qualities, I started to notice that whenever I started talking about my dreams and aspirations, David would ever so cleverly remind me of how grateful I should be for what we already had and reassure me that I would not need to ever do any extra because he would always take care of me. It was flattering at first, but, over time, I started to feel a bit stifled and shut down. We had been married about two years when I finally shared my business dream with him.

It was one evening after dinner, which included all his favorite dishes: barbequed chicken, sautéed collard greens with olive oil and garlic, shrimp scampi with creamy linguini, and to wash it all down, freshly brewed sweetened iced tea. After his second heaping plate, I figured it was a good time to show him my business plan and get his feedback. David held a degree in Finance and worked for one of the strongest financial institutes in New York, so I welcomed and trusted his assessment.

"Hun, I have been working on a little something and would like your feedback. It's not quite finished, but it's my business plan for a bookstore that I would like to open. Can you look at it and tell me what you think?" I asked. My voice was noticeably a little shaky from my nerves.

After skimming through the business plan in a little under five minutes, David responded, "This is nice, but you can't be serious. Bookstores have a high failure rate and African American bookstores are going under every day. I hope you weren't thinking that I would help you fund this *little* project. Have you done any research on this idea of yours Alexia, is there a high demand for a bookstore today?"

I sat there with my head bowed down and my spirit crushed as he continued to verbally slaughter my dream without mercy. "Didn't we just read in the paper that another Barnes & Noble was closing? Alexia, have you not been paying attention to all the reports saying that Amazon is making it difficult for brick & mortar bookstores to survive?"

What David didn't know was that I had done my research. I had also surveyed some local neighborhood people and they had a lot to say about Amazon. Real folks missed going into an actual brick & mortar building to touch and smell the book before purchasing. I don't tell David any of this because I am still in disbelief at how he tried to deflate my vision. "Alexia, surely you could have come up with a better business idea than this."

He threw my business plan down on the table and walked out of the room chuckling and shaking his head. I felt so defeated in that moment, but I also saw a different side of David.

Two months after that evening, I had had enough of his selfish and egotistical ways. I really hadn't paid too much attention to his ways before, but now I was seeing David for the person who he was. It's funny how we see what we want to see in people. This wasn't the first time that I had ignored red flags. When I caught him cheating, he was so manipulative that he had convinced me that his cheating was my fault when I caught him with my own eyes.

David had told me that he would be working some late nights with another associate due to a big project at work. I thought nothing of it since it gave me time to work on my bookstore business plan, and although the other associate was a woman, she had been to our home several times for dinner parties with her husband. We had even had one or two double dates. Lisa was a beautiful and intelligent chocolate-toned woman with a fiery intensity when it came to business. In fact, her and David got into it constantly because he said he thought sometimes she was "too much of a firecracker" and "not feminine enough".

One night, as I was having dinner alone, I started feeling guilty about David working late and eating takeout while I was having a home cooked meal. So, I decided to surprise him with dinner at his office. I even packed enough for Lisa. When I pulled into the company parking lot, there were only a few cars there since it was afterhours, so it was quite easy to find David's car after I parked. As I approached the back of the car, I could see David's silhouette in the driver's seat. I was relieved that I caught him before he left and started walking faster. Halfway there, I noticed another silhouette sitting in the front passenger seat leaned over with her head in David's lap. My heart immediately stopped beating as I came to a standstill. It was Lisa. The paper bag I had been holding fell to the ground, but not before my first teardrop. I didn't know what else to do. I ran back to my car and drove home. I remember practicing what I would say to David when he finally came home, but when I confronted him, he somehow flipped it and said I wasn't giving him enough attention and he had no other choice. So basically, his infidelity was MY fault. It was difficult, but he promised to not do it again and I didn't want my marriage to be over, so I started catering to him more, while I was silently shrinking.

So, after I caught him cheating a second (and last) time, I realized that I wanted more. I deserved more. I deserved someone who would love me as much, if not more than I love me. When I finally kicked David out of the house, strangely enough he acted as if I was overreacting. He apologized and promised to never do it again, but of course, that was the second time I was hearing the exact same thing.

Six months after kicking David out, as I was getting used to the idea of a fresh start, tragedy dealt me the most shocking blow I had ever experienced. Both of my parents were killed in an attempted house burglary. According to the police, two men entered the house through a basement window. Once inside, they were surprised by my father who met them at the top of the stairs after he heard the noise. He put up a fight but was no match for the young men. My mother, who was sleeping upstairs, heard the commotion, called 911 and went downstairs to investigate. She was attacked and hit over the head. She lost consciousness and was pronounced dead enroute to the hospital.

My father was badly beaten and in critical condition when they told him about my mother. He cried until his heart just stopped. This did not surprise me. My parents were childhood sweethearts. Together for over fifty years, I could not imagine one without the other. The two men were caught about two blocks from the house. They were employees of my father. Both men had issues with drugs and thought they could just get into the house and take a few things for a quick sale. They said that no one was supposed to be home. My father had told everyone that him and my mother were going on a long vacation. But, at the last minute, my parents decided to delay their trip by a week.

In that one night, everything about my life was forever changed. Being an only child and a bona fide Daddy's little girl, I was left to deal with the ending of my marriage and the death of both of my parents, who were my number one supporters.

When David showed up for my parents' wake, just like I knew he would because he was always one to try and save face, I had one of my cousins serve him with the divorce papers. To say he was shocked would be an understatement. Even now when I think back to that day, I cannot believe he wasn't expecting those papers. He knew not to try and approach me that day, but soon after he tried to contact me numerous times. With everything else going on, I did not want to deal with David anymore. I couldn't.

My parents had left me everything. I had no idea that my parents had saved so much money. They always preached that "you need to save something for a rainy day." Their home in Long Island was paid for. They also owned two brownstones in Brooklyn where they were collecting rental income. They owned timeshares in Aruba, Mexico and Puerto Rico. Being retired and business owners, my parents did not let any grass grow under their feet. They had always joked that if anything ever happened to them, I would be well off. I just assumed they had insurance policies for a couple of thousand dollars. When Jeffery, who was their lawyer at the time, read each will and informed me that there was a one-million-dollar life insurance policy on each of my parents, I was stunned...

I purchased a brownstone on 139th street between Lenox Ave. and Adam Clayton Powell Blvd. in Harlem. I renovated it to my specifications. *Chocolate, Books & More Café* is located on the lower level, and I live in the two-upper levels. As you enter the front door of my living space you are in a large foyer, which leads you into the living room. Off to the right of the living room I have a sunroom which wraps around the front of the brownstone. Behind the living room is a family style dining room. Off to the left is a den which is as large as the sunroom. The restaurant style kitchen is to the right of the dining room. Off from the dining room you step down into the entertainment room, which is used when I have company. I invested time and money into creating the peaceful and Afrocentric aesthetic I desired. From the Al Jarreau pieces that adorn the walls to the bright colors in the sunroom that come to life in the daytime sunlight, I love the serenity in my home.

From the street, you enter the café by going down four steps. The counter and pastry display cases are to the right when you first walk in. There are ten tables that seat two to four people. To the left in front of the window there is a bar table with six stools. I strategically placed four large comfortable chairs with charging docks built-in throughout the shop. Toward the back there is an area with ten tables, each seating two people. This area I use for private meetings. My plan was to create a warm and inviting atmosphere that everyone would find welcoming and be happy to patronize.

Since it is Friday, which is the busiest day of the week for the café, I run downstairs to begin my daily routine of getting everything ready for the morning rush. I inherited my father's work ethic: "Get an early start on tomorrow today and you will have a productive life."

So, every evening after we close, I start the batter for the next day of muffins. On the menu today, like every Friday and Wednesday, we will have Blueberry, Carrot, and Orange Cranberry muffins. Tuesday & Thursday we offer Blueberry, Chocolate Chip, and Corn Muffins. Saturday, we offer Blueberry, Bran and Corn.

Once the muffins are in the oven, I start the coffee makers and bring in the newspapers that the delivery man has dropped off. Everything is done with an hour to spare. I use thirty minutes to look over the café, like I do every morning, including giving myself a once over in the mirror. I don't ever wear much makeup and today is no different. With my golden locs in a neat high bun, I freshen up my nude peach lip gloss and check my mascara. I smile at my reflection; my bright smile matching the sparkle of my gold hoop earrings, I say to myself "You got this". I sit down in one of the comfy chairs and close my eyes to send up my daily prayers of thanks and blessings to all those who enter these doors today.

Deena and Linda are the only two employees I have. They arrive together talking and laughing. As I watch them, I am sure Linda is filling Deena in on her drama-filled night with this month's boyfriend pick. They are truly God sent. They get along well, and they respect me as their boss. We open the doors thirty minutes later. Deena handles the cash register while Linda takes care of the orders. All morning we have a good flow of customers, and it is not until my stomach starts to growl that I realize I have not had anything to eat. I inform Deena, who has been with me from the beginning, that I am going upstairs to grab something quick to eat and will be back down shortly. I always have my meal break upstairs in my own space. Sometimes it is just to break up the routine of the morning, but since today is Friday and payday for my girls, it will probably be the only time I get a break. So, I will take this time to do payroll. I am reminded that I also need to call Jeffery's office for an appointment. One of the great things about Jeffery is his office hours are usually in the evening. So once the shop closes, I can get over to meet with him.

Deena assures me she would watch everything and for me to take as long as I needed. Just as I am about to walk out, I hear a deep baritone voice that sends a chill up my spine, "Excuse me, can you tell me where I can find the manager?"

As I turn around to tell this person that the manager is out to lunch, visibly annoyed with my head tilted to the side and hand on hip, I lay eyes on a strikingly handsome six-foot God, who looks like he stepped straight out of a movie. His skin is a deep bronze that looks as if he just lays out in the sun all day. His body is proportioned just right, which I am sure is the result of spending hours in the gym. I am momentarily hypnotized by his flattering smile and deep dimples. There is something familiar about this stranger, but if I had met him before, I would surely remember.

"I'm the manager, how can I help you?"

Evan

"Next and last stop is 125th Street and Amsterdam Ave," I say through the bus speaker system. I undo my seat belt and jump out of the driver seat all in one motion. Kevin, the driver who is going to relieve me today, steps up in the bus.

"Hey Evan, what's up? Has it started to get crazy out there yet? Shoot man, I started to call in sick today because you know I hate Fridays," Kevin says. All I could do is laugh before I say, "Kevin you hate getting up and coming to work every day, not just Fridays."

"True, true that," Kevin says as he climbs into the driver's seat and fastens the seatbelt. "Yo before I forget, we are getting together after work and going to Perks for a couple of drinks. You should stop by, even if it is for a minute."

"No can-do homie, I got to work tomorrow," I say as I step off the bus and walk over to the depot to turn in my paperwork for the day. It is times like this I start rethinking my career choices. I have been a New York City bus operator for the last fifteen years. If I worked for the New York City Police Department, I would be retiring soon. Shoot, even if I worked for The Department of Sanitation, I would be looking forward to my retirement now. But no, I had to work for New York City Transit Authority. I started when I was 20 years old. Just thinking about how much longer I must work before I can retire gives me a headache.

My boys are all off on the weekends, so hanging out on a Friday night is common for them. My brother and I own *Brother & Brother Bakery*, so I chose to be off from work Monday and Tuesday. So, once again I can't hang out with the boys. I climb into my Chevy Tahoe and glance down at the digital clock on the dashboard.

"Shoot!" I say as I bang on the steering wheel and mumble under my breath, "One o'clock already." I should have been at the bakery fifteen minutes ago.

Brother & Brother Bakery which we shorten to *B&B Bakery* was my brother Ellis' idea. Ellis was once the biggest kid selling drugs on the corner. After being sentenced to four years in the penitentiary, he promised himself and our parents that he would never get into any trouble again. He made a vow that he would do what he loved to do and pour back into the community that he sold drugs in for so many years. During his time in prison, Ellis got a certificate in cake decorating and a degree in business.

I always loved to bake. I attended and graduated from CAI which is the Culinary Arts Institute in New Hyde, New York. When our parents were killed in an accident, Ellis and I both decided to use the money they left us to do something they would be proud of. We opened *B&B Bakery* on 127th Street and Lenox Avenue. Ellis and I have talked about expanding the bakery business, starting with supplying our baked goods to small businesses in the area. We offer cakes, pies and cupcakes; we also cater small events.

Today is the day that I planned to go over and speak with the manager at the café on 139ᵗʰ street. I will have just enough time to grab the pastry samples I prepared this morning and run over to the café.

I arrive at the café a little after two and there are quite a few customers sitting at the tables engrossed in their phones and laptops. The aromas in the café are almost hypnotic with notes of roasted coffee and burnt sugar. I can even detect the faint, but lingering smell of white sage. The saxophone-heavy jazz music in the background is the perfect volume, soft enough to be heard without being distracting to those working. I can tell the owner has put a great deal of energy into the ambience. Even the Al Jarreau cover art pieces on the walls are of some of my favorite albums. I instantly feel a sense of home.

As I look around, I spot someone who looks as if she may work here. "Excuse me, can you tell me where I can find the manger?" When she turns around, I am looking at the most beautiful woman that I have ever set my eyes on. That face, a face I could never forget. My Sunday morning passenger, who I have been crushing on, is here in the flesh and I am standing in front of her. I am momentarily at a loss for words.

"I am the manager, how can I help you." Her body language clearly indicating she is not in a space to be bothered.

"Let me rephrase," I say with a nervous grin. "My name is Evan Michaels and I own a bakery on 127ᵗʰ & Lenox Ave. I would like to talk to the manger or owner about supplying your baked goods."

"Good afternoon Mr. Michaels, I am Alexia Williams the manager."

"Good afternoon, Mrs. Williams," I say as I reach out to shake her hand. I cannot believe that I am finally meeting the woman I have been secretly in love with for months.

"If you have a moment, I would love to have you sample some of our specials," I say as I raise the basket of freshly baked items for her to see. She smiles softly, looks around and then leads me to one of the unoccupied tables.

"Mrs. Williams, I brought over a few of our bestselling pastries, that I hope you will enjoy," I state as I open the basket filled with an assortment of muffins and pastries. I notice how the scents coming out of the basket mix well with the aromas already in the café, Alexia included...

I grab a few napkins on the way to the table. Whatever he had in that carrier is smelling sinfully good. Or was that him? He definitely looked good enough to eat. Even with the basket in hand, he manages to pull my chair out before taking a seat across from me.

When he opens the basket, I am reminded I still hadn't eaten anything all morning. As I reach for one of the cinnamon rolls, I ask, "May I?" I blush a little as I realize that may have been a bit forward, but I am famished. The cinnamon roll that catches my immediate attention has warm icing oozing all over. As I bite into it, I am immersed in cinnamon and brown sugar heaven- it is flaky, and you get a bit of cinnamon and brown sugar in every bite. The icing is sweet, but not so sweet that it overpowers the pastry, but instead compliments it. As I finish the cinnamon roll, I'm thinking where oh where has this man been all my life because one thing I just love, love, love is a warm, flaky cinnamon roll.

I close my eyes so that I can enjoy this little slice of heaven that this stranger has presented to me. When I open my eyes, Mr. Michaels is staring at me like I have two heads; but seriously, I must have looked very strange to him, eyes closed, and a sinful grin teasing the corners of my mouth. Oh my God, I can only imagine what is going through his mind.

"I'm sorry," I say, "this is very good. Did you bake it yourself?" I had to ask before I began shamelessly sucking the icing off my fingers.

So, here I am sitting inside *Chocolate, Books & More* presenting the basket of treats that I chose specifically since each one is a top seller at the bakery. The blueberry muffin, the apple crumb muffin and then my favorite, the cinnamon roll.

I cannot believe my luck! What are the chances that the young lady that I have been crushing on every Sunday for the past three months would be the same woman that manages *this* cafe? On Sundays, my route is the M104 bus, and I have been picking up this beauty on 125th and Broadway and she gets off at 68th and Broadway. She has never so much as glanced at me to say more than a good afternoon, but I looked forward to going to work every Sunday, just to lay eyes on her.

As I watch Alexia bite into the cinnamon roll with her eyes closed, her eyes do a happy dance behind the lids and the left corner of her top lip curls up ever so slightly. A low moan that is barely audible escapes her mouth. All I can think about is how sexy and desirable this woman is, and how I would love to lick that warm sugary icing off any part of her body.

In order to suppress my manly urges, I take my eyes off her for just a moment and bring my attention back to the artwork on the wall. Al Jarreau is one of my favorite musicians of all time. I still listen to his album, *Breakin' Away*, at least once a week. I wonder if Alexia is into him too or if the owner is responsible for the décor. I want to know everything there is to know about this woman. But first, business…

She asks me if I did the baking, and I know that is my opening. Now if I can get her to convince the owner to give *B & B* a shot at supplying them baked goods, I know they won't be disappointed.

"Can you come by on Sunday early evening?" Alexia asks. She explains that the café is closed on Sundays, so that would be a better time to talk business, and it would also give her time to investigate *B & B Bakery*.

"First, to answer your question, yes, I do the baking. And yes, Sunday works for me," I reply.

"Hey girl, are you up?" I say into the phone as I put on my sneakers.

"Yes!" is my girl LaJune's reply, even though I can detect the tiredness in her voice

"Are you on your way?" she asks. I can tell from the rustling of sheets that she is still tossing around in the bed.

"Yup I will be there in about twenty, so get up," I say as I finish lacing up my sneakers.

"I'm up girl. I'm gonna be ready to go when you get here. I was hanging out after work last night. I met up with someone from the dating app and we had a good ole time," she chuckles.

"Even more reason you need to be walking it off this morning. See you soon," I say and hang up the phone.

LaJune and I have been going walking every Saturday morning for the past three years. We met at a Weight Watchers meeting and found out that we had so much in common from our failed marriages to our small business ventures. I joined Weight Watchers because I have always had an issue with my weight and needed help keeping off the seventy pounds that I lost when I kicked David out. The unhappiness that I felt in that marriage came through in every aspect of my life, even my relationship with food. I had to make some drastic changes and that included my weight and how I looked at my weight. So, when I walked into a meeting and heard this young lady say that she left her husband and left her old self in Atlanta and needed help finding her real self, I knew we would hit it off.

Between recipe swaps and our weekly three mile walks we have both lost weight and been very successful at keeping it off. We also created a friendship … a sisterhood, that we both needed, and it continues to grow and stay strong.

"Good morning girl. I was thinking we should really try to walk an extra two miles today since it is beautiful out. What do you think?" I ask LaJune as she comes down the porch steps.

As I watch LaJune grudgingly walk down the steps, I am amazed at how quickly she was able to get ready. Her long black hair is pulled back into her signature ponytail underneath her Atlanta Braves baseball cap. I laugh discreetly and shake my head as I notice she even had time to apply a light layer of makeup. Who else, but my girl, would wear makeup to go for a power walk? When LaJune gets closer to the bottom of the steps, I get an inexplicable feeling that something is not right. Her eyes appear off. I can't quite place it, but I make a mental note to ask her if she is okay. Knowing LaJune she will say she is fine, and nothing is wrong, but looking at her, I am convinced something is going on with my girl.

"Girl, you know it is really too early for your jokes," she says with an open-mouth yawn that she doesn't even try to stifle.

"Would you believe that David has finally agreed to sign the divorce papers," I state more than ask as we come to the last round of our power walk. I go on and start telling LaJune about the early morning phone call and my visit with the lawyer yesterday.

"Finally! I wonder what happened to make him come around after all this time?" she asks shaking her head in disbelief.

"According to the lawyer he wants to just go on with his life and put the past behind him," I tell LaJune.

"I don't buy that. He fought you for so long, especially after he found out about your inheritance and then was hating because you had the nerve to open your own business," LaJune says as we round the bend.

"LaJune, the café is my true baby. Something that he felt should just be a hobby. I worked hard to get the café up and running. When other businesses were closing all around me, I put my all into my dream and he just couldn't understand that. I really don't know what his problem was but I'm glad he figured it out and I can now go on with my life."

LaJune says, "Speaking of going on with your life, are you now ready to start dating? You know it would serve David right if you found someone else, someone who treats you right and makes you very happy. Alexia you are beautiful. Skin flawless and you don't even wear a lot of makeup. And that au natural is the *in* look today. Your smile lights up any room you walk into. You have so much to offer the right man."

I turn and look over at LaJune and once again I am reminded why I love this chick so much. She always knows what to say and just when to say it.

"Girl, he thought I couldn't make it without him. He just knew I would come crawling back to him. He said so many hateful and nasty things to me the day I kicked him out. He was acting like I was the one who ruined our marriage."

"Look, I don't want to talk about David any longer," I say, ready to shift my energy.

"Speaking of meeting someone new, I had a strange visitor in the café yesterday morning, a Mr. Evan Michaels," I share with my girl.

"Wait a minute, do you mean Evan from B&B on 127th?", she asks

"Yes why, do you know him?"

"Girl who doesn't know the drop-dead gorgeous brothers who own *B&B*. Evan is the youngest and if I say so myself, the sexiest. The older brother Ellis, I believe is the brains behind the whole operation."

"So, missy how did you meet Evan?" LaJune asks with a little too much enthusiasm.

He came into the café yesterday asking for the manager so he could present his pastries and request that we consider using their bakery as the supplier for various baked goods.

"And why you didn't tell him that you are the owner and do all your own baking?" she asks while looking at me all crazy.

"No, I didn't, but I will when I see him tomorrow. We have an appointment for tomorrow afternoon."

"Do I hear a little excitement in your voice about your meeting?" LaJune asks with a wide-eyed grin.

"I don't know about all that, I mean I don't think I'm excited … but there is something familiar about Evan and I can't quite put my finger on it."

As we end our walk back in front of LaJune's brownstone we kiss, left cheek then right cheek, and then a hug- our usual parting ritual.

Evan

"So, Lil' Bro tell me, how did it go yesterday over at the cafe?" Ellis asks as we sit in his office going over the weekly schedule. With me working full time for NYC Transit, the bakery schedule allows me to do my share and not get burned out. We have one full time baker, two part-time student bakers and two young ladies at the front counter. Ellis handles the many office details and the administrative duties. When we have a catering job, Ellis likes to work on the baking then.

Ellis has always been extremely intelligent and business-minded, even when we were younger. He even applied that same intellect when he was dealing drugs, before he went to prison. Even though I knew what he was doing was wrong, I was always in awe watching him talk to his faithful customers. He would be on his corner at 116th and 8th Avenue educating the younger boys, telling them to stay in school and not be in the streets.

Seeing him sell drugs was confusing to me at first. I didn't understand why he couldn't just use those smarts in school. Over time, one thing I learned about my brother was that he was a natural entrepreneur who needed his independence and, until he found other outlets, that's what selling drugs gave him.

Our parents were heartbroken when he was arrested after an anonymous tip resulted in an undercover sweep. Ellis was in the wrong place at the wrong time, and he was swept up as well. I missed my brother so much when he was in prison. I had never seen our parents so deep in sadness. Surprisingly though, no one was more heartbroken or sadder than Ellis. He knew he disappointed our parents and felt like he let me down too. This motivated him to make use of his prison time and he got his degree, but his guilt only multiplied when our parents were tragically killed while he was locked up. He was released not long after and we both decided to make our parents proud by using the money they left us to open *B & B Bakery*.

"I met the manager and she agreed to meet with me tomorrow. I will let her know about all the jobs we have and how we will be an asset to her café."

Just thinking about seeing Alexia tomorrow has me sweating and I can feel my nature rising. Thinking about the effect the cinnamon roll had on her and what I would love to do to her with some warm icing has me enkindled. I stand up and walk to the other side of the office and turn my back to my brother. I don't think I would be able to explain a visible hard on created by just talking about this woman, Alexia.

"Oh, Ellis did I tell you that the manager happens to be the same woman that gets on my bus every Sunday morning?"

"What … are you serious? Did she recognize you?" Ellis asks as he walks over to me and hands me my mail that comes here instead of my place.

"No, I don't think so. I really don't think she even notices me when she gets on the bus. She gets on, dips her MetroCard, and sits in the middle of the bus, and when I get to 68th & Broadway, she gets off through the rear door, without even noticing me or saying a word."

"Damn, bro you got it bad," Ellis says laughing so hard that some of his thick locs fall out the hair net and down his back.

"So, wait, how are you going to have a meeting with her tomorrow, isn't tomorrow Sunday? And don't you have to work?"

"She said she will call me today to set up the time for me to come by, but I am sure it will be after she goes to wherever it is I drop her off at."

"Ok well I hope everything works out for you tomorrow because I know you have been discussing doing business with that café since they opened. Let me ask you something Evan," Ellis says as he taps his pen on his wooden desk, something he only does when he is unsure about something. Ever since we were little, and Ellis was trying to figure something out he would tap on the table or whatever he had close by. Daddy would tell him that that is how he knew Ellis was going to take over the world one day. His *tap, tap, tap* would allow him the time he needed to get his thoughts right. His choice of words would be precise and deliberate. Ellis would never be considered impulsive.

"Have you ever patronized the café? I mean have you been a customer and tried her muffins or her chocolate cake?" Ellis asks me.

I look at my brother and I start thinking back before I answer, because one thing I know for sure is that he would not ask a question like this unless he is sure of the answer.

"No", I answer. "I don't think I ever have. Why, have you?" I ask my brother with my eyebrows raised because he has never mentioned that to me.

"Of course, I have, when it first opened. I stopped in to satisfy my curiosity. I really enjoy their coffee. She also has a great selection of books that she updates regularly. The vibe is inviting and comfortable, so much so that I go in there about three times a week".

"Really," I say, "Why have you never mentioned it?" I couldn't help but to ask.

"Honestly bro I was waiting for you to tell me that you did and what you thought of the bakery items," he replies.

"So, tell me, are the muffins good?" I just had to ask.

"Yes, I must admit they are. They have a blueberry crumb muffin that would make you want to slap somebody. They also have a chocolate-chocolate chip muffin that is also scrumptious."

"So. Ellis, tell me do you think I am wasting my time meeting with her?" I ask, feeling a little somber.

"No, I think you should go meet with her. Take our portfolio, include a few customer reviews and a couple of samples from the menu that you think will add to her café. Then you may just have a shot."

"I actually took a sample of the cinnamon roll when I went by yesterday, and she loved it!"

Now my mind goes back to her reaction as she was tasting the roll. Alexia Williams is a very sexy woman even when she isn't trying to be. I can't help but to wonder how she tastes. I probably would enjoy her just as much as she enjoyed that cinnamon roll.

"Thanks bro," I say as I walk over to give my big brother a hug, before I leave his office. Before I go through the door I turn back and smile at my big brother and I say, "See that is why you get paid the big bucks because you are always thinking."

All he could do is laugh and tell me to finish up the order for the *S & S Book Club*.

One thing I can always count on is Reverend Edwards' sermon speaking to my heart and giving me something to carry me through another week. As I am on my way home, I reflect on another beautiful Sunday morning service. Every Sunday morning, I attend the 8:00am worship service at Unified Baptist Church in Hempstead, Long Island. People always ask me why I travel so far to attend a service. I live in Harlem, the home of New York's Historical Black Churches, but I need to attend a church that feeds my soul and leaves me thirsty for more. The young pastor Edwards does just that every Sunday. Unified Baptist is not a church that performs for the cameras or tourists, like so many of the churches in Harlem today.

"I'm not judging I'm just saying," I say to myself chuckling. I swear I crack myself up sometimes.

So, while I'm driving home on the Southern State Parkway, I can't help but to think about his message today: "Wait on the Lord and be of good courage." I start replaying the whole Sunday service in my head and before I know it, I am home.

As I enter the foyer I glance up at the clock and notice the time is 10:20. Great! I still have enough time to make my egg white spinach omelet and enjoy a good cup of coffee. I have not been the best at managing my time on Sunday mornings. No matter what I do, I could never have breakfast before I leave for church.

I go up to my bedroom to change out of my clothes and into one of my many jogging sets. I love these sets because they are so comfortable. They are very versatile; you can dress them up or down depending on your mood. I choose a purple one.

This is what I enjoy about Sundays. The day that is truly just for me. From the spirit-filled church service to a tasty omelet and an invigorating cup of coffee. "What could be better?" I whisper to myself. "Well yeah maybe Mr. Evan Michaels sitting across from me." Wow, where did that come from. Well, I will see Mr. Michaels soon enough. I called him yesterday to set up our meeting today and we agreed to meet at 4:00 this afternoon.

As I get up to place my dishes in the sink, I realize it is now 11:15 and I have just enough time to walk over to St. Nicholas Ave. and then over to 125th and then to Broadway. I will get my 12:15 M104 bus, which will take me to Barnes and Noble on 68th Street & Broadway.

s I step up on the bus and use my MetroCard to pay my fare, I hear the usual "Good Morning" and like every previous Sunday I respond with a mumbled "Good Morning." I never look up because it's common knowledge that NYC Transit workers are players, especially those bus drivers. All you need to do is look at them and smile and just like that they assume that they have another admirer. So, you will never have to worry about me, Mr. Bus Driver. I will speak, but I will not give you the satisfaction of looking at you.

After my dry "Good morning", I ease my way down the aisle toward my usual seat. But something catches me this morning. There is something familiar about that deep baritone voice. Nah it can't be. Now I'm scared to look for other reasons.

"Good morning Mrs. Williams," I hear and now I stop in my tracks and turn around, blocking the flow of people entering the bus. "Excuse me miss can I get by?" an older woman behind me says with an obvious attitude as she pushes past me.

"Yes, I'm sorry" I say as I step to the side and start to walk back to the front of the bus.

"Evan? What are you doing here?" I can't help but to ask, but immediately feel silly since it's obvious that he's driving the bus.

"'How are you?" he asks, grinning like a schoolboy.

"I'm well," I reply but I can't help myself, so I ask again "Evan what are you doing here and how come I have never seen you before?"

"This is where I work, and I don't know why you have never seen me. I have been picking you up every Sunday for the past three months," he states.

"You drive this bus *every* Sunday?" I ask.

"Yes Alexia, you get on and sit in the middle and then you get off at 68th and Broadway."

"Really," is all I could say as I am preoccupied with noticing how muscular his arms look in his blue uniform shirt. I also notice how easily he maneuvers this 40-foot bus and find myself fantasizing about how well he could maneuver me.

I sit down in the first seat to the right of the driver, which becomes vacant right on time as I find my knees weak being this close to Evan. I just could not believe I had missed seeing his gorgeous face for 3 months. "Evan, I can't believe you have been driving this bus every Sunday and I didn't notice you."

"Well," he starts, "in your defense you are always so engrossed in whatever book you are reading to notice anything around you. A couple of times you were so preoccupied that I would be at the bus stop for a few seconds before you realized it was your stop. I would even announce the street three or four times before you would jump off."

We both laugh as I remember the exact times he is talking about. As I look out the window, I realize we are approaching 75th street. I wonder if we are still meeting this afternoon because he didn't say he had to work today.

So, I ask, "Are we still meeting this afternoon?" I pray it didn't come across as desperate as it sounded to me

Evan glances over at me as he stops at a red light, his eyes having their own conversation with mine and says., "Yes, I will be there at four o'clock as promised."

And it was then I realize that I was holding my breath and I release it slowly as to not draw attention to myself or pass out. Dang, how did we get here so quick. I look up and notice we are at my stop. As I exit the bus, I thank him for a nice ride and say, "I will see you later." To which he replies, "Yes, you most certainly will."

While walking to the Barnes & Noble for my creative writing class taught by New York Times Best Selling author Dee H. Hollis, I notice my heartbeat quickens and the hairs on the back of my neck are tingling. My thoughts are on Evan and the way he was maneuvering that bus. I remember looking down at his hands on the steering wheel and wondering if he could guide his hands across my body with the same smooth control and expertise. I smile and giggle to myself at the mere thought. "Whew, yes it has been a long time," I say to myself as I walk into the Barnes & Noble.

It is so difficult to concentrate in class today. My mind keeps drifting to Evan. I can't believe that I have never noticed him before today. Dang, the way that uniform shirt hugged every ripple in his chest and abs. That man is fine!

"Alexia is everything okay?" Dee asks me. "You just didn't seem like you were here today and that is not like you," she adds.

"Dee, I apologize, I have a meeting this afternoon with a supplier, and I guess I was just a little preoccupied thinking about that."

"Alright girl, just remember we only have two more weeks for the class and your short story is due next week."

"Yes, I know girl. Alright I will see you next week and I promise to be more focused," I say as I say a silent prayer for the same thing. Dee says, "Ok, next week, we shall see." We both laugh at our little secret. Dee has been coming into the café every Wednesday morning for her caramel latte and chocolate chip muffin. Dee is also a member of *S& S Book Club* which holds their monthly meeting at the café.

*O*nce I get home, I retreat into my sanctuary which also happens to be my bedroom. When I bought this brownstone, the first room I had renovated was the bedroom. I wanted to create a soothing relaxing haven with enough open space to allow the natural sunlight from the large bay windows to illuminate the space with light and warmth and give life to the teal and silver decor. The room also has a nook which I turned into a reading area. It is large enough that I have a comfortable chaise and a bookcase that wraps around the left wall. On the right wall, I have my collection of African American artwork. On the center wall I have an electric fireplace, which adds to the intimate setting that I desire when I spend time reading and writing. The room also has a hidden sound system installed because I love listening to Anita Baker, Al Jarreau, Toni Braxton and even some Kenny G when I am in my solitude. Before you know it, it is time for me to get ready for my meeting with Evan.

Once I take my shower, I decide to put on a pair of brown linen capri-style pants with a tan blouse and some brown wooden Ankh earrings. I gather my locs up into a top bun to accentuate the earrings and the blouse. I apply a touch of my favorite Mac Revealing lip gloss, and to my pressure points I add some lavender vanilla body oil, which I make myself. I go down to the café to put on a pot of coffee, some light jazz and start the diffuser while I wait for Evan's arrival.

Evan

I decided to make a few apple crumb muffins and some chocolate turnovers, which I'm sure she will love. Both items are on the "most wanted" list among customers at the bakery. Once I put all the paperwork in the briefcase and sit it by the door, I go up to take my shower. My thoughts instantly go to Alexia and the way she looked earlier today. The surprised look on her face, the hint of a smile and the gleam in her eyes the second the recognition occurred. And I know I was not imagining the quiver in her voice when she asked if we were still meeting this afternoon. I'm not sure what this woman has done to me, but what I do know is that I cannot stop thinking about her, her face, her body, her beautiful blond locs that accentuate her mocha hue … who says black women shouldn't wear blond!

Today, when she got on the bus in that purple jogging suit and Reeboks, she looked so sexy and cute. It took everything in me to keep my eyes on the road and not her thick thighs and shapely behind.

Thank God I am in the shower because as I am thinking of Alexia, my nature begins to rise. My first thought is, "This Nivea men's body wash will come in handy", but then I realize that I don't want to do this. When I finally get with Alexia, which I know it will happen, I want to give her all of me. I do not want to exert all this energy on pleasing myself in this shower. So, I do the next best thing and turn on the cold-water full blast to ease some of this frustration.

Once I come out of the shower I put on a pair of jeans and a simple white Chinese-collared shirt, and since this is a business meeting, I add a black chef's jacket with the name *B&B Bakery* embroidered on the left corner. I opt out of spraying on my favorite cologne. I want Alexia to only inhale the aroma of the pastries and whatever natural pheromones I'm giving off.

I decide to walk to the café because on Sundays in Harlem, parking is very scarce and once you have a spot, you keep it.

When I arrive at the café, Alexia opens the door, and I can't believe she is more beautiful now then she was earlier. How could that be?

"Hello," I say as she lets me in and closes the door behind me. I hand her the traveling case, "I made more pastries for you to try so you can tell me what you think."

"Ok great," she says. She tells me that she has put on a pot of coffee, and she offers me a cup. She walks with the pastries to get our coffee and what my eyes are privy to immediately makes me hard enough to cut diamonds. The way her linen pants hug her hips and accentuate the curvature of the arch in her back is hypnotizing to say the least.

We make our way to a table and sit down, and she puts a muffin and a turnover on the table in front of us along with our coffee.

"Why don't you tell me a little about *B & B*? But I must warn you, I heard some stuff through the grapevine," Alexia tells me with a smirk.

I tell her about Ellis and the time he spent incarcerated. I share with her how our mother taught us to bake and how that was all we ever wanted to do. I told her how long we have been in business and why we chose Harlem as the home for our bakery. I went on to tell her about our clientele. The first being a woman I met at a small business seminar we attended looking for clients. Her name is Tamiko Evans, and she has a small non-profit organization for young girls called *P.E.T.A.L.* which stands for *Positively Empowering Teens About Life*. She holds conferences for teen girls. At each conference we provide her cakes or cupcakes and if she is going to do breakfast, we provide all the pastries. Another client just so happens to be Tamiko's husband. He owns his own photography studio company which is called *One Eye Shutt*. Along with photography, he writes and shoots short stories and films. When he has a photo shoot, he calls on us to supply the baked goods. He has done all the photos we use for our advertisements. *One Eye Shutt* also shot our commercial that is shown on a Harlem cable channel.

"Alexia, as you can see, most of our business is word of mouth. Which I think is a testament within itself," I add hoping to cinch the deal.

"Impressive, I have heard of Tamiko Evans. My girlfriend held a workshop at one of her conferences, a couple of months ago," Alexia says.

"Would you like another cup of coffee?" she asks as she fixes herself one.

"No thank you," I reply. "Now that you know about *B&B*, tell me a little about *Chocolate, Books & More*, starting with how long you have been the manager."

"Well, for starters" she says with a grin "I am the owner and manager."

So, we both are laughing, and I ask her, "Why didn't you correct me?"

Wow, I can't believe I missed that. In this age of Google, I can't believe I didn't Google the café and find out that Alexia was the owner. This may cost me, I think to myself.

"Evan, you asked for the manager, and I am she," she says with a grin and bow of her head.

"I opened *Chocolate, Books & More* two years ago. I am the sole owner and I do all the baking myself. I have a passion for reading and bringing people together."

I can see the passion she has all over her face as she is explaining her business to me, but I can't help but think of what other kinds of passion she enjoys.

"There is nothing better than getting lost in a good book while sipping on a rich creamy hot cup of coffee or steamy cup of tea," she continues. She pauses and suddenly stops talking. I can see a faraway look in her eyes as she seems to be looking past me. Before I could say anything, Alexia shrugs, quickly regroups and continues.

"My plan was to open a little storefront strategically located by a bus stop. A place you could wait for the bus when the weather was severe. I had wanted to open it up in Queens, but circumstances beyond my control brought me to Harlem."

"This was just a shell when I acquired it and now look at it. Evidence of what a little hard work and determination will do."

"Wow! Now that is what I call impressive," I say. "Do you think that having someone else do the baking will help or hurt your business?" I ask as I reach to refill my coffee mug. I had declined earlier, but now I feel parched from being so turned on.

"I'm not sure but I am willing to give it some thought. Freeing up the baking will allow me the opportunity to concentrate on the *books* part of the café, which is my true passion," Alexia says

"Alexia, I must ask how did you come up with the name? It is very catchy"

"I love chocolate and reading. They are my sinful pleasures. The *More* part comes from the other things we offer. We also carry little trinkets like bookmarks, magnets and mugs."

"I would love to open the café for more small intimate meetings, preferably reading groups, and book launch parties. I have the space for it. I incorporated that very possibility into the design," she tells me gesturing to the back of the cafe.

"You have done a wonderful job in making the café inviting and comfortable. When I walked in the first time, even though it was bustling with customers, it was very cozy and intimate. Between the jazz that comes through the sound system, the Al Jarreau album cover artwork and the delicious aromas, the ambiance makes it very difficult to leave."

"Thank you, Evan, that is exactly what I wanted to create," Alexia replies with pride.

The room got still and quiet and I am thinking I need to say something. Just then Alexia, reading my mind, continues. "So, tell me how long you have been driving the bus?" Alexia asks this with a crooked grin. I am sure she is thinking back to our earlier encounter just as I am.

"I have been working for Transit for fifteen years now."

"You must be getting ready to retire right?" she asks, impressed.

"Unfortunately, not, I started when I was twenty. They have very strict rules concerning time worked and age of retirement. In my case I have time but not the age."

"I really have been staying there for the pension to be honest with you. The bakery is doing well, and Ellis and I are committed to the bakery and its success. What we have been discussing, is the option of me freezing my pension and working full time with the bakery. For the moment, it is just a thought."

"Smart move, Evan. You can't go wrong with having a pension and you will still be relatively young."

"Yeah, that is the same thing Ellis says, especially when you are an owner of a small business."

Alexia and I continue our conversation talking about our lives and passions

"Wow," Alexia says as she glances up at the clock on the wall. "Evan, the time just flew by. Have you realized we have been talking for hours, the pot of coffee long gone and the delicious treats you brought over are gone also?"

Before I could say anything, my stomach made a very embarrassing sound and we let out a laugh.

"Alexia I'm sorry, I did not realize how late it was. I was enjoying getting to know you a little better."

"Thank you, Evan, I was enjoying the same. I didn't get a chance to cook any dinner but if you would like to stay for dinner, I could order something, and have it delivered."

After a Thai style dinner and a couple glasses of wine, our business meeting begins to feel more like a first date.

As I look over at Alexia, I can't help but to notice how truly beautiful she is. Just naturally beautiful, without the need for any enhancements or makeup. It is that natural beauty that only a Black woman can exude; her high cheek bones and sexy full lips and her alluring dreamy eyes seem almost hypnotic. She is wearing a sweet vanilla scent that has been teasing my senses all evening. It must be working as an aphrodisiac on me because I cannot think of anything other than tasting her lips.

My heart is beating so fast and hard, that I hope it is not noticeable or audible through my shirt. I close my eyes and shake my head to clear it up and try to get some sense of clarity. But when my eyes open Alexia is leaning over to me and she has placed her hand over mine and is saying "Evan, Evan, are you alright?"

I'm unable to answer her due to the lump that has formed in the center of my throat, so I decide to speak with my actions instead. I do what I have been wanting to do since I saw her this afternoon on the bus; I lean into her, and I kiss her slowly and passionately. I kiss her again, a little deeper this time. I cup her face with the palm of my hand, and I kiss her for the third time. This time I try to convey all the need and desire that I have for her. I wanted this woman badly since I laid eyes on her months ago, and the fact that I had just officially met her two days ago adds to my urgency and excitement of having her. When I finally pull myself away from her and I look into her eyes, what I see makes my heart sink.

"Alexia I am sorry," I say, dropping my head a bit.

"I didn't mean to upset you," I say as I gather my things and push myself away from the table.

"Evan, I'll look over all of this and give you a call when I have come to a decision," she says with what seems to be touch of irritation.

I was hoping her first words after the kiss would have been telling me not to leave.

I walk myself to the door and turn back to look at Alexia, who is still sitting at the table, not even looking in my direction, and I say, "I'll be waiting to hear from you, goodnight."

While walking home I reflect on what just happened. Why did I kiss her?

This is a rhetorical question to myself because I could give a whole dissertation on why I kissed Alexia. I kissed her because that is all I could think about from the moment I stepped into the café. I kissed her because her aura is so captivating, and it almost holds me hostage in her essence. I kissed her because she radiates sensuality. I kissed her because I wanted to feel her lips on mine, I wanted to explore the warmth of her mouth with my tongue. I wanted to taste her.

As I toss and turn in my bed that night, my thoughts are on Alexia. I wonder what she is doing, did she enjoy the kiss, and will she forgive me…

I know I wanted Evan to kiss me, but when he does, I get tongue-tied. Speaking of tongues, that kiss was unbelievably amazing.

Initially I was caught off guard by his actions. Was I sending him some signals that I wanted him to kiss me? These are the thoughts that are racing through my head as I lay in the bed tonight. We were having a good conversation and then suddenly he got this dreamy, spaced out look in his eyes. He closed his eyes and started shaking his head. I thought he was having a seizure or something. Not sure what to do, I just softly said his name, and when he didn't respond, I called his name again and gently squeezed his hand. When his eyes opened, I did not have a chance to say anything because he was then covering my mouth with his.

As I lay here remembering his kisses, I can't believe what is happening to me. My body is reacting to just the thought of Evan's kisses. A warm sensation is taking over my body, my nipples are hard and there is an uncontrollable throbbing going on between my legs.

Sleep will not come to me tonight, so I do the next best thing. I do the only thing that helps me release. I hit the treadmill. I turn on the sound system and of course it's Mary J reminding me it's *MY Life* and I begin to walk off some of this sexual frustration.

On or about the third mile I start asking myself, why didn't I ask him to stay? Why didn't I tell him I was enjoying his kisses? Why could you not just let go and live in the moment and let that man know you were feeling him? Who am I kidding? I know all the answers. "Thank you, David for damaging me!" I scream out to an empty room as I slow down and get off the treadmill.

I take a shower and realize that I am still wired from earlier today and it is now midnight. So, I decide to get a glass of Moscato and begin writing my short story for class, due in two weeks.

Whew! I can't believe I have been at this computer for three hours writing. It's as if a fire has been ignited in me and my creative juices are just flowing. I think I will try to get some sleep now because not only did I finish the bottle of Moscato, but my short story is also complete. I will do some editing on it later in the week, but for now it is a done job.

"Girl if you don't slow down, you are going to have to call EMS for me. I am going to pass out right here in Morningside Park!" LaJune says as she tries to catch her breath.

"I'm sorry LaJune," I say. "I am just so frustrated and upset. You know walking helps relieve some of the stress."

"What has David done now?" she asks, as we slow down.

"No, it's not David, I haven't heard from him or his lawyer since the last time. It's Evan Michaels."

"Oh," she says surprised and intrigued at the same time. "Things aren't working out with him doing the baking?"

That's right I'm thinking to myself, I have not been able to fill her in on what happened at our meeting, so she must have assumed that I hired *B&B* and that my frustration was business related.

"Girl, I need to fill you in because we have a lot to catch up on." It has been a couple of weeks since LaJune and I have been able to get together. "Girl, you have been doing so much overtime and we have not been able to even go walking."

So, I tell her about getting on the bus and Evan being the driver. I share with her that he said he had been noticing me for months, but I hadn't even noticed him. Even though there was something familiar about him, I would not have made that connection. I then shared about the meeting and how everything was going well because I was really considering taking him up on his offer. I then told her about the kisses, but I purposely left out how good it felt, and how I wish he had not stopped.

"Girl shut your mouth before a fly goes straight in for a landing," I say to her because she is standing there looking at me with her mouth wide open.

She stopped walking and turned to me with wide eyes and an even wider grin and asks me, "So how good was it and did y'all take it any further?"

I could not believe she was asking me that. Well, yes, I can. I guess she knows me better than I give her credit for. "Girl it was good," I reply with a *sistah girl* laugh, "but that was it". I try to explain what I think must have happened. I continue by telling her that I have not called him since that night. When she asks me why, I look at my BFF and tell her, "I think I'm feeling this man that I just met about two weeks ago! How crazy is that?"

Evan

"Hey bro," I say to Ellis as I bust my way into his office. "I think you are right the second week in July is perfect to close for a two-week vacation." Ellis had come to me with a calendar asking me when I think we should take vacation. He explained how it would be best to take two weeks together and we both could go on vacation and this way neither one of us will be stuck doing the work at the bakery during that time.

"Do you also have those weeks for vacation with Transit?" Ellis asks

"Yes," I reply, "That's why it will be perfect. And it will be a late birthday present to myself." Ellis rolled his eyes, smirked and then went straight into business mode.

"Evan, we have been doing really well this past year with the new clients and the possibility of adding the catering extension to *B & B*, I'm really excited. So, what's going on with Alexia Williams? Have you heard anything from her yet?" he asks.

I had told my brother everything about our meeting. I even

expressed to him how I made a fool of myself. His only reply at the time was give her "some time and see what happens." So, I guess the time is up, since he's bringing it back up.

"No, I haven't heard anything. I am a little surprised. I thought she would have called and at least told me she would not be doing business with us, but I haven't heard a peep."

"Well," Ellis hesitates. "Don't you think it is time you contact her? And I would suggest you keep it professional by going by the shop during normal business hours, to see if she at least gives you the time of day."

"Yeah, I will," I say as I play it out in my head. With a café full of customers, she shouldn't feel threatened by me.

"Ellis," I say, "Can I ask you something?"

Ellis chuckles. "You never have to ask for permission to ask me anything," my big brother says with a puzzled look.

I wipe my forehead and nervously continue, "Do you think I messed up by kissing her?"

My big brother looks up at me, removes his glasses which he only wears when he is going over the books and throws them on the desk. He places his elbows on the desk, entwines his fingers and places them under his chin

"Evan, you are so much like Mom that it is not even funny. You wear your emotions on your sleeve just like she did. Dad always said that was one of the things he loved about her. I don't think you messed up. You could never mess up when you let your feelings be known. Now did you scare her, maybe, but the fact that she hasn't called, I would take as a good sign. Baby brother don't ever stop being you. There is a woman out there that would love you for being you and this Alexia Williams may just be her. Now, if I may, can I ask you something," Ellis says with a smirk and a side eye. "Are you in love with her?"

"Bro, I have been in love with Alexia from the first day I set eyes on her. When she got on my bus that first time and then when I stepped in the café that day, I could not believe my luck."

My brother shakes his head, puts his glasses back on and says, "Well I guess you'll be heading over to the café sometime during the week."

Alexia

hree weeks have gone by, and I finally decide to contact Evan. I did not see him on the bus this past Sunday when I went to my last writing class. So, I'm thinking I must have really blown it with him. Just as my head starts having a pity party for my crazy thoughts, I hear that deep voice that instantly stops my heartbeat.

"Good morning Mrs. Williams. How are you?"

I look up from the tray of chocolate brownies that I am putting in the display case.

"Good morning Mr. Michaels. I am fine, how are you?" I ask as my heart begins to beat again.

"Did I catch you at a bad time?" While he is talking to me all I can do is think about what I can do to keep this man from running out of the same door he just entered.

"No, actually your timing is perfect. Let me just finish putting these away and we can have a seat and talk."

"Hey LaJune," I say through the phone when LaJune picks up after the fourth ring.

"Hey Alexia, what's going on?" she replies.

"Not much, I am in the mood for some apple martinis and wings. Do you feel like hooking up and catching up?"

"Sure, give me twenty minutes to get ready." In "LaJune time", I already know that means more like forty minutes.

"Ok, spill it," LaJune says after about our third round of apple martinis. LaJune looks effortlessly beautiful tonight. I could tell she spent extra time sleeking her signature ponytail tonight. Her makeup is a simple glam and flawless.

"What makes you think I have anything to spill, my dear friend?" I say, blushing.

"Alexia, If I know one thing about you whenever you want to talk, we go for a walk or we go for martinis and wings. Now spill it!" she says impatiently and then takes a long sip of her drink.

I can't help but to laugh at LaJune because she is so right, and she knows me so well. It is times like this that I can't believe we have only been friends for a few years.

"Alright, alright," I say.

"Evan came into the café yesterday and apologized for kissing me. He also asked if we could do the meeting over."

"That's a good sign. So, what did you say?"

"I told him there was no need to apologize and there was no need to do the meeting over."

Before I could even finish LaJune screams out, "Girl, you better tell me you didn't!"

"LaJune, will you let me finish!" I scream back at her to shut her up. "Long story short *B&B Bakery* will be providing baked goods for the café starting Monday. And yes, I agreed to go out on a date with Evan," I squeeze out at the end. LaJune is beaming with joy like a proud mommy who just watched her baby take its first step.

At the same time our server approaches and asks if she can get us another round.

We look at each other and laugh. That is the beauty of living in Harlem; everything is in walking distance or a cab ride away. So yes, we both say we'll take another drink and another order of wings. I immediately feel guilty, but LaJune is right on time as usual, reading my mind.

She winks and then says, "We can walk it off in the morning."

"Ok girl lets have all the juicy details," she says as she downs her martini.

Alexia

It has been raining off and on since last night. Listening to Lonnie Quinn of CBS News give me permission to stay in all day is exactly what I need this morning as I roll over and sink further into my king size bed. The pillow top mattress and my plush luxury bamboo pillow envelope me like a hug. Deeper and deeper I sink until I snuggle into a comfy spot. *Ahhh,* Monday mornings. I treat myself to one day of sleeping late and just relaxing for a couple of hours before I get the day started.

I hear that annoying buzz from my phone, indicating I have a notification. I consider not even checking it, but I decide to do the responsible adult thing and half heartily check my phone.

> *Gm gurl, will be there about 9 with breakfast*
> *Fish and Grits and mimosas of course.*
> *Luv ya*

This is exactly why I love her. And then I realize she must have taken the day off. Oh dang! I say to myself while laughing because if my girl is coming over, I will not get anything done today.

True to her word, at nine o'clock LaJune rings my doorbell. She walks through the door, arms loaded down with bags. "What is all this?" I ask, as I try to grab some of the bags to help my girl out.

"You said breakfast. This is way more than breakfast," I say as we walk into the kitchen and start unpacking bags. The girl has even managed to pick up my laundry. I side-eye her.

"I know, I know," LaJune says. "But what had happened was," she starts, and we both just crack up laughing at her improper use of the English language.

After a delicious breakfast of fried fish, shrimp and cheese grits from my favorite spot, we sat at the table full and satisfied. I went to reach for the champagne to fix us another mimosa and I could not hold it in anymore.

"Okay, spit it out. Why did you take off from work today?" LaJune does not take days off from work. She prides herself on having a perfect attendance. So, something is terribly wrong, I'm sure.

Before she answers me, I notice that she seems to be uncomfortable. She shifts in her chair. She is wringing her hands together. She hesitates for a moment, clears her throat and then in an instant she is back to her confident bubbly self.

"*Gurl,* I just felt like hanging with you today. We haven't really been able to hang because of our schedules."

I am shaking my head in agreement, but I know something isn't right.

"Alexia, I know you. You would have stayed in bed late. Then jumped up around noon running around trying to squeeze in everything you had on your to-do list."

Yes, I nod again in agreement. I am starting to hate that she knows me so well.

"So, I did what friends do. Picked up your groceries and your laundry. Got us some breakfast and morning cocktails. All so we can have some *sistah* gurl time." She says all this as she is waving her hands in the air and moving her head all around.

I roll my eyes and apologize for thinking there was an ulterior motive behind her morning visit.

"LaJune, must you really be so dramatic?" I ask her as I throw one of the napkins at her face.

I glance at her sitting at the opposite side of the table. I cannot shake the feeling that something is not right with my friend.

I silently make a promise that when she is ready to talk to me about whatever it is I will be here.

The morning turns into afternoon, which is quickly turning into evening. We have caught up on our shows Law & Order SVU and Criminal Minds. We both sit in shock as Derrick leaves Criminal Minds and vow never to watch the show again.

LaJune suggests we order Chinese food. "Why ruin a perfect day by cooking?" she asks rhetorically as she dials our favorite take-out spot.

As we enjoy our dinner of Shrimp and Broccoli, Shrimp Egg Foo Young and of course Shrimp Fried Rice, LaJune asks, "Have you ever thought about relocating?"

I look up at my friend and try to see where this question came from.

"Me, relocate?" I ask, puzzled at the random question.

"Yes, would you or could you just pick up and leave and start from scratch", she asks.

"Yes, I would go someplace where it is hot all year round.

Cause girl I am so done with shoveling snow." I laugh and then say, "Seriously, I have thought about it to some degree. Opening another café would most definitely be in the plan." I begin telling her and then it hits me. This must be what she needs to talk to me about. My girl must be thinking about relocating again. I say again because she relocated here from Atlanta. Which I am very grateful for because that is how I was able to meet her. Something must really be going on with her for her to be considering moving again.

So, I finally ask, "What's up girl, is everything ok with you? Have you started dieting again because you look like you are losing weight?"

"Everything is fine," she says. "With the crazy hours, I have been putting in, my eating habits have been very crazy," she explains

I look at my friend and accept her explanation but make a mental note to talk to her again because something just isn't right. I can feel it. We finally call it a night at around nine o'clock. We had a great day. The time just flew by. After LaJune leaves, I get comfortable and hunker down to call Evan. We have been talking every day and night and it hasn't all been about business. On Mondays, we usually communicate via text messages until the evening when I am free. I notice that there are at least 6 missed text messages from him. I read them all before I dial his number, a smile plastered on my face.

Alexia

Ring, ring, ring

I know my phone is not ringing at 4:30 in the morning. What the hell is going on with these early morning phone calls, I think as I roll over and pull the comforter over my head.

Ring, ring, ring

For real, this better be important. "Hello" I say, my annoyance plastered all over my groggy tone.

"Alexia, this is David please don't hang up the phone."

"David?! How did you get my number?" All our correspondences have the café address and number.

He doesn't respond, so once again I ask,' "David how did you get my number?" My sleepiness now replaced by anger.

"I thought calling you was safer than coming into the café."

I nod my head in agreement. "You were right. But really, why are you are calling me at 4:30 in the morning? I guess it would have been too much to ask for you to call at a reasonable hour." Mind you, he still has not answered me about *how* he got my number.

I am now out of bed and pacing in my dark bedroom. This is the effect that David has on me. It would be just my luck that David just happens to call me now. Evan and I have been going out for the past month. We have done breakfast, lunch, and dinner. We have enjoyed going to the movies and been getting to know each other. There have been a lot more kisses. Yes, wonderful breath-taking kisses. This is what is on my mind as I hear, "Alexia, Alexia are you there?"

"David please don't call me. Whatever you have to say to me you can say it to my lawyer," I say as I hang up the phone.

I cannot believe that David had the nerve to call me. Of course, I am now up and won't be going back to sleep for a while. I decide to go downstairs and fix myself a cup of tea. I have a special tea blend that I only fix when I need a real take me away moment. And if there was ever a need for me to escape, this morning is the time.

The last time I felt like this was almost four years ago. That day it was raining hard, and I woke up with a headache. I realized that it was my sinuses acting up causing a sinus headache. I went to work and did my best to try and complete a full day. As the day went on, the rain came down harder and nothing was helping my headache. After a few hours I decided to go home early and get in the bed and just ride it out. As I put my key in the door, I could hear Miles' horn coming through the speakers. Hmm, David must not have gone to work today, which was a surprise, but I remember just thinking, "Oh well". As I put my wet rain gear in the foyer and hung it up, I noticed a green Ralph Lauren raincoat that I had never seen before hanging up where my coat should've gone. Maybe it was my headache, but I truly didn't even give it a second thought in that moment.

I prepare a cup of tea and I sit down in my oversized loveseat with my knees curled up to my chest. I wrap my hands around the hot steamy mug and down memory lane I continue as my thoughts travel back to that day.

The CD player must have been on automatic play because this Miles CD I know by heart. When I came in the last song was ending and it is now playing the first song on the CD.

I climbed the stairs that lead to the bedroom and the upstairs bathroom. My headache and the torrential rain outside temporarily forgotten, I wondered who that green raincoat belonged to.

When I got to the top of the stairs, I smelled something, like Jasmine or a honeysuckle plant. I glanced down at the outlet that was in the hallway. The outlet was empty, so the smell was not coming from an Air Wick air freshener that I usually kept in the outlets.

Just then I hear something that rocked me to the core.

"Ooh yes Daddy that is how I like it. Come on baby you got my spot. Yes, Daddy that is what I like."

With my next breath caught in my throat, I walked into my bedroom undetected. I stood watching in horror as I watched my husband having sex in our marital bed.

I gasped loudly still trying to get some air into my lungs and just then the woman opened her eyes and looked right into mine. She jumped up pushing David off her in the process. "David, oh my God, David!"

My husband turned around, looked at me and said "Alexia, what are you doing home?" Not even trying to cover himself, he repeated "Alexia, what are you doing home?"

I cannot believe what I walked into, in my house, in my bed.

This girl was running around my bedroom looking for her clothes. Clothes, which at that time, I noticed were spread all over the room. My husband stood in front of me as naked as the day his Momma brought him into this world, and he asked me again, "What are you doing home?" as if I was the one who had explaining to do.

I can recall that entire scene like it was yesterday. Homegirl running down those steps and fumbling as she was trying to put her clothes on, and she tripped and slid down the steps. I laugh at the memory but laughing was the furthest thing from my mind in that moment.

In *my* house, in *my* bed. The audacity!

"Alexia, Alexia," I heard David calling out my name.

I had lost my voice. I was speechless. There had been so much I wanted to say to David in that moment, but the words would not come out.

"GET OUT! GET OUT! GET OUT!" I screamed.

"GET OUT NOW!"

I shudder as a chill runs up my arms thinking back to that horrible day. My tea is finished, and I realize that I need to get down to the café. I cross my arms across my chest and rub my arms vigorously to knock off the chill. Hearing from David seems to have stirred up all those feelings again. Feelings, that for so long, I have fought hard to bury. This day is not off to a great start.

1 2:30 is what the clock above the coffee machine reads. This has been one of the busiest mornings in the café. I am exhausted. It could be from being up since 4:30 this morning. After that trip down memory lane, I could not go back to sleep.

"Alexia, there is an Evan Michaels on the phone," Deena whispers in my ear as she relieves me from the cash register.

"Hello, Evan, how are you?" a slight smile forming on my lips.

"Good afternoon, Alexia, I am fine now that I hear your voice. How are you, Beautiful? You sound drained."

Blushing, I respond, "Busy and tired but I guess that is a good thing. Evan, what do I owe the pleasure of this call?"

"Alexia, I know you and I know you probably did not have anything to eat yet today. So, I was going to drop a salad by before I head over to the bakery."

This is exactly why I am falling for this man. He always has my best interest at heart and knows what I need. I can't help but smile and shake my head. "Thank you so much, Evan." I then tell him to knock on the office door if he does not see me on the floor.

"May we have another round of chocolate martinis please?" I ask the waitress.

There is nothing better than spending time with my girl. LaJune has just returned home from a family reunion trip. When she called me as soon as her plane landed and said she needed a martini and some wings, I just knew that something went crazy on her trip. So here we sit about to indulge in our second round of martinis.

"Girl, I'm telling you my mother has lost the little bit of sense she has left," LaJune says as she reaches for a wing.

"Girl you not even right for saying that," I tell her as we share a laugh. It probably should not have been funny since her mom is suffering from senility, but her comical tone plus the effects of the martinis made it hard to take anything seriously right now.

LaJune shares with me that her mother had her home attendant send an invitation for the family reunion to her ex-husband.

What she couldn't understand was why he accepted the

invitation and showed up for the trip. He even had the nerve to try to say he wanted them to share a room. What he said was, "You know your mom thinks we are still together so what could it hurt if we share a room."

LaJune shares what happened that first night and the weekend just kept going downhill after that. Her mom kept referring to him as her son in-law and asking them when they were going to make her a grandmother. LaJune and I laughed so hard over the whole thing. Then I let her cry on my shoulder as she talked about her mother losing her memory and her guilt about not being there with her mom during this time.

We must have made our server nervous with the whirlwind of emotions going from laughing to crying, because she sends over the manager to check on us. "Ladies is everything ok?"

I just nod my head to let him know that everything is fine. "May I have some coffee sent over to your table?" I guess he thought that we had had too much to drink. I am sure before approaching our table he asked our server how many drinks we had consumed.

"Yes, thank you. we would like some coffee," I finally replied

We were not that bad.

Evan

It has been extremely busy at the bakery this week with Ellis out of town looking into possibilities of opening another *B&B Bakery*. I have been pulling double duty at the bakery this week and I am so looking forward to my two-week vacation. The bakery will be closed, and I am off from the bus operator duties. Since I acquired the café account, I have been coming in early every morning to get their order out. I would not dare leave the baking to someone else. "The timing of this vacation is on point," I say to myself as I pick up the phone to call Alexia.

After a much-needed conversation break with Alexia I am feeling energized and ready to take on the rest of the day. I go out to check on the front of the store to make sure everything is cool. Ellis and I lucked up when we hired Chrisette and Anita to work the front of the store. They both are excellent in customer service, and they do not mind hard work. It is a bonus that they were friends from the neighborhood. As I do a walk around, I pick up some trash that was left on the tables and wipe down the few that are not occupied.

I also take the time to speak to the customers and thank them for their patronage.

"Well, if it isn't boss man, he done came out to be among us common folks"

I cannot help but to laugh as I greet the mailman, Dan. "What's up Brother, how's things?"

"I can't call it bro; I'm still here pushing this here mail cart."

"Man, I'm glad you are because you know I know how your co-workers be slacking," I just had to throw into the convo.

I ask Chrisette to give me two apple turnovers and tell Dan to follow me to the back.

Dan and I talk and catch up for almost an hour. We have been friends since elementary school. He started working for the post office right after college. So yes, he will be retiring real soon. Since we opened the bakery, he does the bulk of his area before he gets here. Today this works out well because we can hang out while he takes his lunch break. We talk about everything from sports to cars. I ask Dan how his mom is doing since she has moved in with him. Dan turns his head and looks at the floor as he takes his time to talk about his mom. "Man, she apologizes every day for ruining my life. It breaks my heart that she thinks she is trouble for me."

Dan's dad passed away when we were young, and his mom became mother and father overnight. A few years ago, his mom had a stroke and Dan did not think twice about moving her into his house. She feels she is in the way of his happiness. He feels that he can finally repay her for being the best mother a child could ask for.

We give each other our signature brotherly hug and he leaves to finish his mail drops for the day.

When Dan leaves, I go through the mail. Nothing of importance, except for one envelope. I put most of it in a nice pile and leave it on Ellis' desk for him to deal with upon his return. The one envelope I take, I put it in my pocket so that I can deal with it later. I then decide to check on emails and other things before the girls need me out front.

Evan

"What do I owe to the pleasure of your visit Jazmyne?" I say, immediately regretting opening the door for her. My day was going well and I was looking forward to listening to this new jazz CD I purchased today.

Do I really want to know the answer to that question? I truly do not. The last time Jaz and I were together, she stormed out of the same door she just walked in. Looking at her standing in front of me, I am reminded of the last time she was here.

"You will be sorry E, that I can guarantee you. You will never find anyone to love you like I do," she had said as she pulled the front door closed behind her. She had used so much force that a frame that hung on the wall near the door went crashing to the floor with a loud bang. How ironic that the same frame that was then on the floor with all the glass shattered, held the quotation 'Don't Leave Without Kissing Me Good-bye.'

"Evan, I told you I will always be around and will pop up at any time."

Jazmyne, the 5'2 self-absorbed ball of fire, was born with a silver spoon in her mouth and golden slippers encrusted in diamonds on her tiny feet. Jazmyne always had to be in control, always wanting to be in control of her life and mine.

"Jazmyne, I mean what are you doing here, now? I thought you were still jet setting all over the world." I could not resist throwing that in. I hate the mood this woman puts me in.

"I was missing Harlem and of course you and all the fun we used to have," she said with all the added drama: seductively fluttering her eyes and speaking with a low purr. I always hated when she did that. I couldn't believe she had just said that with a straight face. So, I just shook my head and chuckled to myself.

"Are you still driving the bus?" she asks with no real interest at all. The question is basically rhetorical. She rolls her eyes and makes a sucking sound with her teeth and lips, letting her condescendence be known. Jazmyne always thought that anyone having to work for a living was so beneath her.

"You know, Evan if you would've stayed with me, you would be traveling the world while someone else does all the manual labor," she says as she flops herself down on the sofa in my living room. "You are not going to offer me anything to drink?" she asks as she removes her clearly high-priced jacket.

I am not surprised at her brashness; she makes herself comfortable without noticing I have yet to offer her something to drink. "If you have something preferably cold and bubbly, that would be awesome," she continues. As I find something in my kitchen for Jazmyne to drink, I can't help but to shake my head at how she just shows up at my door. Being with her always left me feeling like I was a charity case. She was always trying to take care of me in the most demeaning ways. She had been trying to plan out my whole life, which would include her of course. When she found out both my parents had died, it just seemed to fuel her on her path to becoming my parent.

The real Jazmyne is a spoiled stuck-up brat. And that is the reason why I couldn't be with her. Her acts of kindness are never genuine; they're only tools of manipulation.

As she sits there drinking her orange juice, I can tell by the perturbed look on her face that she's offended that it doesn't have any Moet champagne added.

"I came by because you never answered any of my letters. And I know you would not ignore me if I was in your face," she says with that cunning smirk she is known to use.

"Evan I just got back into town and Mommy and Daddy have been asking about you and want you to come to dinner. Mommy also said to let Ellis know because she wants to see him as well."

"Jazmyne it was great seeing you," I say, mostly as a courtesy, as I stand up and start walking to the door, hoping she gets the hint and joins me. She takes her time getting up off the sofa, but she does and leisurely walks over to me at the door after grabbing her jacket.

"Evan please come to dinner tonight. I have missed you so," she purrs. "I wrote you to tell you I was coming back home. I even called the shop a few times looking for you," she starts whining. "I really have missed you, Evan" she says as she grabs for my arm and rubs up and down my forearm. The space between us gets smaller and she wraps her arms around me. "Come to dinner tonight baby, I will make it worth your while and give you a proper birthday present."

"I'll talk to Ellis and call you later," saying anything at this point to get her out the door. The fact that she tried to use my birthday as part of her ploy makes me cringe even more.

Once I close the door, I start thinking how ironic that Jazmyne shows up now, now just when things with Alexia have been going so well. In my head I hear Jazmyne's whiny annoying voice. I never realized before how annoying her voice was or how irritating her touch is.

Alexia has the voice that commands respect. It is soft, but strong. It is comforting and it embraces you like a warm hug, not purring and shrilly like Jazmyne's

"Ellis come on man answer the phone," I say through clenched teeth as I wait for my brother to pick up his cell phone.

"Hey Evan, what's up?" Ellis says as he picks up the phone

"Ellis, you will not believe who stopped by here today?"

"Who?" Ellis asks, but by the way he says it, I am sure he has an idea.

I fill Ellis in on my recent visitor and we both agreed that going to the Jones' home for dinner would not be a good idea. Even though it would be great to see Mr. & Mrs. Jones, unfortunately Jazmyne would also be there and that would not be great.

Ellis never cared much for Jazmyne. When we were younger and then when she attached herself to me and started treating me like her property instead of companion, he cared even less for her.

Evan

Today went by way too fast. I even forgot it was my birthday. After my unexpected and very much unwanted visitor, I decide to make the day the best that it could be. It is now eight o'clock and I have been sitting at this computer all day. Being on vacation from work this week, I decided to catch up on some new recipes and research any new business ventures Ellis and I may want to go after. The loud grumbling sound that comes from my stomach reminds me that I have not eaten anything all day. For some reason, Alexia crosses my mind. I immediately smile at the thought. And even though I would love to call her up to ask her to join me for a birthday dinner, I decide to enjoy an evening alone in my man cave.

My man cave is a brownstone on 137th Street and Bradhurst Ave. that was given to me by my parents. My parents purchased three brownstones when they were being offered in a lottery for one dollar each. Not too many residents of Harlem at the time saw the upraise that was going to happen in Harlem. So, they slept on the opportunity to own a piece of the pie. I live in one and my brother Ellis lives in the one next door to me. The other one is located on 140th Street between Bradhurst and Frederick Douglas Ave., which we use for rental income. I gutted the brownstone out until it was nothing but a shell. I hired my homeboy Smitty who owns his own contracting business to do all the renovations. I wasn't very particular about the details but the kitchen and living room had to be specific to my wants. The kitchen has full marble countertops with gray and black accents throughout. All the appliances are stainless steel. I took great pleasure in designing the kitchen I wanted, thinking I would be spending much time here. In the living room there is an all-brick mantle fireplace which takes up one corner of the room. The walls are painted a deep rich taupe with mahogany flooring in the living room. The furniture that I chose had to be manly and comfortable which, for me, equated to worn and rugged leather-like microfiber. The sofa has two end pieces that recline, and a middle section that will hold a bowl of chips and up to four mugs. This way when the boys come over for game day, everyone is comfortable and there is no fighting over my big game day chair. My chair is a big recliner that takes up a corner by itself. It has a pocket for the remote, books or magazines and the arm rest has a slot that my Yankees mug fits into perfectly. All of this sits in front of my 52-inch flat screen TV mounted on the wall. In a console under the TV sits my entertainment center which holds a Blu Ray DVD player a Boise CD changer with an iPod dock station all in one. I may be one of very few people who still uses DVDs and CDs. And all of this is hooked up to a wireless surround sound system with speakers all throughout the house. Unfortunately, the only time I really get to enjoy all of this is when I am on vacation, like now.

While making my homemade pizza dinner, the soothing sounds of an up-and-coming artist, Naiqui MaCabroad, is helping to change my mood and making food always puts me in a calm and creative space. I start by chopping onions, green peppers, dicing tomatoes and mushrooms, shredding the cheese and finally browning the sausage. I grab a Corona out the fridge. There is nothing better than having an ice-cold corona in my Yankees frozen mug.

Pizza and beer on deck, good music and of course a game playing on the big screen TV with the sound on mute.

"This is the perfect way to kick my vacation into gear. Happy Birthday to me," I say to myself as I wait for the pizza to be done. I am really enjoying this CD. I need to go online and check this young cat out and see if he has anymore music out. His style has notes of jazz, which is different.

I can even see Alexia playing this in the café, I thought. "Whew, where did that thought come from?" I ask myself.

Alexia and I have been spending some serious time together. After the first time I kissed her and made a fool of myself, I vowed to be patient. I waited so long for her to notice me. Now I finally have her in my life, I cannot seem to get enough of spending time with her. Everything about her is just perfect. Her bronze skin, her golden locs, her sexy shape. It is getting harder and harder to control myself around her, but I will wait, no matter how long it takes.

For some reason, I think back on that unexpected visit from Jazmyne I had earlier today. Saying I was surprised would be a great understatement. I can only hope that Jazmyne does not make a habit of just dropping over.

Jazmyne was the one who taught me how to take care of a woman. She showed me how and where to touch any woman to bring her to the height of an orgasm. Being with Jazmyne was all about the sex. There was no romance, no showering with affection, just heart thumping, ground shaking sex. I never thought of a future with her. My mind was always in the present, the here and now. Whenever Jazmyne would bring up a future together, I would change the subject.

"Evan," she would say. "You will never find anyone that rocks your world like me. We belong together." Jaz was right about one thing; she rocked my world. She knew that I craved her sexually, but it was all the other stuff that came with her that I didn't want any part of.

Jazmyne and Alexia are as different as night and day.

As I gulped the last of the Corona in my mug, I decide to end these thoughts of my past.

"Perfect," I say as I take the pizza out of the oven and place it on the counter. Just then the buzzer for the front door goes off and I look at the security monitor.

I don't believe who is standing in front of my door. This must be the day of surprises. I look at the pizza on the counter and then at the monitor again. My birthday just got that much more interesting.

"Hey," I say as I open the door and lean on the door frame with arms folded across my chest. "What a surprise," I say

Alexia is standing at my front door looking delicious in her sweats. She looks good even when she isn't trying to.

"I'm sorry I have been calling and haven't been able to get you. I was in the neighborhood so I figured I would just come by." With a chuckle she then says, "I know that sounded corny but it's the truth. I didn't catch you at a bad time, did I?" she asked.

"No, no of course not. Come on in," I say as I move over to allow her to enter my apartment. "I'm sorry Alexia, where are my manners, please come in and have a seat," I say waving my hand toward a sofa as I run through the living room to get the remote to turn down the volume on the music.

As I return to the living room, I explain how due to the volume I never heard my phone ringing. I then also explain that the phone could have still been on vibrate from earlier today when I was trying to get some work done.

"I just whipped up a pizza for dinner, would you like to join me?" I ask, but wondering why I would ask her that since this evening was supposed to be about enjoying my time alone. I enjoy her company, but sometimes a man just wants to be alone with his beer, music and sports. Regretting the thought just as quickly, I know why I offered her to join me for dinner. Deep down I was excited she was here.

"You made pizza, or did you take it out of the packaging and place it in the oven?" Alexia asks, while giving me the side-eye.

"La mia donna," I say as I hold out my hand for Alexia to take. I then lead her into the kitchen.

"What did you just say"? Alexia asks while following me.

"'La mia donna' means my lady in Italian. Since you will be entering my Italian bistro, I wanted to do it right."

Shaking her head and blushing, Alexia says, "Wow you are full of surprises."

"Now would you like wine or beer with your pizza?"

After Alexia glances around the kitchen and narrows in on my empty mug, she replies, "I'll have what you are having as long as it's Corona with a twist of lime."

"Wow, I am truly impressed," I say as I take my empty plate over to the sink. "Evan, that was so good. When you said pizza, I just assumed you meant frozen. I was wrong."

"I don't get the chance to cook often, but I enjoy it. So, when I am on vacation and don't have to be at the bakery I will usually cook," he responds.

Hmmm, I immediately start wondering if he's as good in a bed as he is in a kitchen.

"Would you like to go into the living room? We could watch a movie if you like," Evan asks, thankfully interrupting my illicit thoughts.

"Sure, can I take my beer?" I ask.

"You know. I must admit, you do not look like a beer person," Evan says

"What does a beer person look like?" I ask as I follow Evan back towards the living room.

"I really don't know but you just look like someone that prefers a glass of wine if you are going to drink at all." Evan says as he is looking me up and down trying to size me up.

"I like to drink Martinis. But with pizza or a juicy cheeseburger a cold beer is a perfect match."

"What about you Evan, what do you like?" I can't believe I said that. I was doing so good now here I go. I can only hope it goes over his head.

Nope, he caught it too. I can tell from that smirk that flashes across his face and that dark look in his eyes.

"I like a cold beer, but every now and then I enjoy a good cognac," he says after a brief pause.

"I also like having you pay me a surprise visit, especially on my birthday," he says as he rubs the side of my face with his hand. He moves his face so close to mine that not even air can pass between us. "I like the way my hands feel on your face," he says.

Before I can say anything, which would've been hard to do since my breath was stuck in my throat, his mouth was over mine and sharing his breath with me. Evan was giving me life through his kisses. His tongue caressed the inside of my mouth, first tenderly and a hint of apprehension, and then with fiery fervor and desire. The intense heat and craving that was threatening to consume every part of my body needed to be extinguished.

From the first day I met Evan I knew he would be the only one that could put out this fire, because he is the one who ignites it.

He takes a break from sucking on my bottom lip to whisper in my ear that he likes the way his tongue feels in my mouth. The throbbing sensation I feel climbing up the inside of my thighs lets me know I made the right decision by paying him a visit. I didn't even know it was his birthday.

"I want you Alexia," he says, his deep raspy voice dripping with lust inciting parts of me to drip as well.

His hands caress my body as he strategically and effortlessly unbuttons my blouse and lifts my bra over my breasts. He does all of this without ever letting his tongue leave my mouth.

Evan stops sucking on my tongue long enough to plant passionate kisses down my neck. He grabs one of my breasts in his strong manly hands. As he massages my breast, he looks deep into my eyes.

What I see in his eyes makes my heartbeat even faster. Instinctively, my legs spread wider as I sink deeper into the sofa.

I close my eyes trying to stop my head from spinning.

Evan takes one of my breasts in his mouth and then the next one.

"I cannot take it anymore," I whisper in his ear. Just then, Evan lifts me up and carries me up the stairs. I don't have time to take in the beautiful decor in the room or the spiral staircase he just carried me up. What I do notice is the king-sized bed that he has laid me on.

Alexia

After removing all my clothes, Evan steps back to take me all in. The look that he gives me does not make me want to pull the covers over my body, my usual response to being looked at naked. His look exudes lust and a burning desire. When I look into his eyes my body aches for his touch. He pulls his T shirt over his head and throws it across the room. He lets his jeans fall from his waist and my eyes widen as I now take him all in, as I wonder if I could really take him *all* in. I say a two-fold silent prayer: first, that he doesn't hurt me and then 'Thank You God!'

"Alexia, are you sure you want this? I will be gentle."

Instead of answering him I wrap my arms around him and pull him close to me. I kiss his lips and ease my tongue into his mouth. I begin to make love to his mouth, and I don't hold back. I suck on his bottom lip and then run my tongue over his full mouth. I take a break to catch some air and just long enough for him to reach into the night table and get a condom that he has in the drawer. Once he is properly protected, I open my legs to invite him in.

He attempts to enter me and is met with a little resistance. "I won't hurt you baby," he whispers in my ear.

"Let me love you," he croons as he places his hands under my buttocks and raises me up to receive him.

He thrusts forward slowly and then again slowly. The third time he thrusts deeper, and I gasp.

"I'm sorry baby, do you want me to stop?" he asks in a heavy voice.

I push my body up to take him all in and move my hands to his behind and pull him deeper. into me.

"No baby please don't stop. Ooh baby ooh baby don't ever stop"

"Alexia, you feel sooo good, better than I ever dreamed."

This can't be happening is what I'm thinking. I must close my eyes because the whole room is spinning. "Oh, my God, Evan, oh my God, Evan!" I begin to scream out.

"Yes Alexia, cum for me baby, give me all your loving," Evan moans in my ear as he begins to thrust harder, harder, and faster as I become more and more moist.

I let out an earth-shattering scream and Evan's body stiffens up as he lets out a deep moan.

In one motion, Evan rolls over and pulls me to him and cradles me to his body.

I close my eyes in the safety of his embrace and all I can whisper is, "Happy Birthday Evan".

ight feather-like kisses on my naked back cause me to open my eyes.

"Well, hello sleeping beauty," Evan says as he continues to trace the middle of my spine with kisses, not missing a single vertebra. My back arches in response, ready for more of him.

"Good morning," I whisper as I turn to face him and make sure he took the time to put on a condom. Satisfied and turned on by his thoughtfulness, I turn on my side and open my legs to receive his throbbing manhood that was pushing up against me. Even after the three times we made love last night, I take him inside of me as if it is the first.

"Oh, what a feeling" is on repeat playing in my head. The sensation that engulfs me is like a running faucet that is turned on full blast. Evan turns me around, so we are face to face. "I want to look into your eyes as you explode," he says. "You are beautiful, so beautiful while you are in ecstasy."

We roll over and I am now sitting on top of him. As I move, I place my hands on his chest to slow him down and let him know that it's my turn. I do not want him to do any more work. I want to please him and ride him as if my life depends upon it. As I move my hips and squeeze my thighs together, Evan places his hands on my waist as we rhythmically and simultaneously increase the speed and intensity of my thrusts.

"Yes, baby, yes Alexia," Evan pants as the veins in his forehead begin to bulge. His chest muscles tighten and his legs begin to shake. He can no longer lie still; he begins to pump his body up into mine. He holds me tight and with one final upward thrust, "Agh, agh" he says as I collapse on top of him.

I lay there basking in the glory of our early morning love making session. I truly cannot remember a morning as beautiful as this.

"What is on your agenda today my fair lady?" he asks as he comes out of the shower still damp. I can't seem to get enough of this man. Just looking at him sends a wave of desire rippling through my body. I can feel my nipples start to harden and I begin to throb between my legs. I cannot believe I am feeling this way after the night we had and then the session this morning.

"Oh my God," is all I can manage to say in a low whisper.

"What did you say?" Evan asks.

"I'm meeting my girlfriend today for some lunch and long needed girl time," I tell him as I get out of bed and head to the bathroom.

I ask him if I can take a quick shower. He says of course and informs me he will go down and start a little something to feed the appetite we worked up this morning. He laughs as he bounces out the room.

Once showered and dressed I realize I better give my girl a call because knowing her she is probably worried sick about me. I had spoken with her before I came over to Evans house and she told me to call her once I got back home. When I came over here last night, I had not expected for the evening to turn out the way that it had, but I surely ain't complaining!

Lajune

anging out with my girl is one of the parts of my life that I enjoy the most. Martinis and wings and of course a slice of cheesecake makes my living worthwhile. I met Alexia soon after I moved from Atlanta. I was at a bad place in my life, and I knew I needed to make some changes. Since I secured my job before leaving Atlanta, the next thing for me to do was to find a Weight Watchers location so I could work on my weight. I had always been pleasantly plump. While married to Eric I must have gained close to one hundred pounds. My marriage only lasted ten years but the damage that it did to my self-esteem would last a lifetime.

I would work all day and then go home to cook my husband a full course dinner every night. And of course, when he didn't come home for dinner, instead of letting the meal go to waste I would eat his plate after I ate mine. While waiting for him to come home, I would munch on chips or cookies until I would get tired and fall asleep.

On the weekends I would plan for us to do something exciting together. Unfortunately, it would always end up with me in the house alone and in front of the television with a bowl of chips on my lap.

Before you knew it, I couldn't fit into any of my clothes and resorted to sweats and anything with an elastic waist.

He started complaining about my weight and staying out more. I started eating more. He started calling me fat and sloppy. He let it be known that he was no longer attracted to me. He would tell me all I could do for him was to please him orally. He would often say that he could not make love to me because the sight of my body turned him off. His constant badgering and degradation played a huge part in my instability.

I knew he didn't love me anymore when he allowed his mistresses to call the house and he would carry on conversations with them in my presence.

I put up with that for a couple of months because honestly, I felt I let myself go and who else would want me. I convinced myself that it was my fault he was cheating in the first place.

One night he was on the phone and was telling the person on the other line that his wife wasn't home. About an hour later the doorbell rang and he answered the door. I stayed in the bedroom because I could not believe he could do something so wicked.

Music was playing and a lot of laughter was going on downstairs in my living room. I knew it wasn't any of his boys because they would usually go in the man cave, which is in the basement.

In that moment, I had to take a long hard look at myself and my life. Here I am in a self-imposed lock-up in my very own bedroom, while my husband is entertaining his other women in my house.

Something came over me and I had had enough. Oh, hell to the no! I'm going down there and will throw them both out.

I get up and walk to the door and then I turn around and sit back down on the bed. Who am I fooling? I am not going to go down there so they both can laugh at my pitifulness.

is company must've been here for about an hour when I finally hear him come upstairs and knock on the bedroom door. He tells me to come downstairs. He wants me to meet someone.

Ok, maybe I was wrong; it couldn't possibly be the next chick. Even he wouldn't want me to meet her, right? He wouldn't be that cruel, right?

Well, yes, he would and yes, he was.

I go downstairs and when I enter the living room, I knew I should've stayed upstairs in the safety of my bedroom.

"Lynn this is LaJune my wife." She jumps up from the couch and says, "I thought you were joking when you said your wife was home."

She looks at me, confused and apologetic, and says, "I'm so sorry. I thought he was joking"

"LaJune this is my friend Lynn." He says as he rubs his hand across Lynns' back

"Can you get us something to drink?" he asks with a smile.

I turn around and go into the kitchen with tears streaming down my face because I can't believe my life has come to this. Firstly, because this Lynn character is not what I would have expected- she is taller than me, but I am sure she weighs about the same as me. She is not a skinny chick. She is what they call thick. It looks better on her I guess because of her height.

While I'm in the kitchen Lynn comes in to see if I need any help. I shake my head and wave my hand at her dismissively. I can't even utter a single word. The words wont form in my mouth.

She puts her hand on my shoulder and apologizes once more. She then tells me that she doesn't understand why I put up with this from him. She shrugs her shoulders and walks out of the kitchen.

The rest of that unbelievable evening I chose not to remember. Whatever the reason, I believe I do that so that I can survive.

It took me two months to line up a new job, an apartment and to move everything out of the house I shared with Eric.

He had no idea what I was planning because for those two months I was rarely home. I had taken leave from my job so I could do job and apartment searches at the local library. When a company required an in-person interview, I would schedule it on a Friday or Monday. When he noticed I was home in the morning when I should have been at work, I explained it by saying they adjusted my hours for training classes. I chose New York because where better to get my life back than the great Big Apple, the city that never sleeps.

The changes I made to my life were just as dramatic. I threw myself into eating right and working out. Since I loved to eat all the bad things, I knew I needed help, so I joined Weight Watchers

My best friend, Alexia is the one who helps me even when she doesn't know it. I know she would be disappointed in me if she knew my little secret. But this little secret is the only thing that helps me through moments like this.

Moments like this when I start going down memory lane. Reliving all that negativity and pain has a way of creeping into my life. It always seems to take me back to that time in my life when I had no self-esteem, no self-worth.

Funny how now it seems I can mask it well. Well, mask it well enough to fool all those around me.

As I arrive at the restaurant, I notice Alexia's car is already here. I chuckle to myself because that girl will never be late for wings and drinks. I find her at our favorite table, and she is engrossed in a heated conversation on her cell phone. The server comes over and I am happy to see it is our usual girl, Lisa. "Hey LaJune, can I get you the regular?" she asks

"Yes Lisa, thank you," I reply.

Alexia finally hangs up the phone and I can tell she is not very happy.

"What's up girl? Who the heck was that?" I ask as I take a sip from the Martini that Lisa has placed in front of me.

"Please," Alexia says as she rolls her eyes and waves her hand to let me know she doesn't want to talk about it. "What has been going on with you lady?" she asks, trying to change her energy. "I swear it seems as if we can't work out our schedules to get in any walking" she states.

Agreeing, I then fill her in on the latest with my job and how I was once again looked over for a promotion. I explain how I didn't feel bad about it. I was just tired of the nonsense.

I glance at Alexia and notice for the first time since sitting down the beautiful glow that is coming from her face. I smile and ask her "What, my dear, has you beaming so brightly?"

As Alexia picks up a wing, she explains the source of her happiness.

"Evan, he makes me so happy," she says, her voice almost un-recognizable with joy. She goes on to explain, "We have been having so much fun together in this short period. Girl we even went bowling. And you know how I love to go bowling and can't bowl a lick. To be honest he is just as bad as I am. But the fun that we have is crazy," she says right before she chuckles about something that she keeps to herself.

We are finished with our wings and two martinis apiece when I finally bring up the phone call that she was on when I arrived. "Who was that on the phone?" I ask again.

"That was David. For some strange reason, he has taken to calling me a little too often for my liking. I really don't like him calling but I feel like something is going on."

"Something like what?" I ask her.

"I can't quite put my finger on it, but it is something," she says.

As we prepare to leave, I excuse myself to go to the ladies' room.

It takes me less than twenty minutes to finish in the ladies' room and I head back to our table.

Upon my return, Alexia asks, "LaJune must you always brush your teeth after every meal?"

I am a little taken aback by her question, but before I could reply she says, "That's what you told me you do every time you go to the bathroom after we eat. You said you can't stand the aftertaste of food in your mouth."

Recovering quickly, I chuckle and laugh it off. "Girl, I told you I like to be prepared for whatever, or whoever because you never know who you may run into."

"That is why I will always keep gum or mints in my bag," I remind her. And then I place a Breath Saver mint in my mouth as I pass her the pack. She waves me off and says, "Girl you know I don't like those things; I like real peppermints."

We both just laughed and hugged each other with promises to see each other soon.

Now let's see if Evan is as predictable as he has always been. Yup, three steps from the bottom, two bricks from the right and shake the brick just a bit.

"When will he ever learn," I say to myself as I take the key from its hiding place. Evan has been hiding an extra key here for years. Ever since the day he left all his keys on his bus in a haste to complete his shift, he decided to hide a spare key somewhere outside. As I struggle in the door with an armful of bags, I can't help but giggle. Evan is going to be so surprised. I have been back in New York for two months and he has not been by to see me. Every time I call the bakery, Ellis says he is not in. Those brothers are thicker than thieves, so I am sure Evan was right there each time I called.

I know I have been gone a long time and didn't write Evan often, but I missed him. There is only so much partying one person can do. You get tired of drinking all night and waking up with someone and you don't even remember his name.

It was on one of those mornings that made me realize I had a good thing back home. Evan wasn't impressed by my family name. It didn't matter that my father was one of the wealthiest men in the world.

If only he would've just let me take care of him, we would be together now.

I picked up his favorite dish from Tony's Restaurant in Long Island. Baked Shells filled with extra cheese and with meat sauce, mozzarella garlic bread and a side order of steamed spinach. I put everything in the oven to stay warm. I put the wine in the fridge to chill. I know this is going to blow his mind because he really thinks I can't be domesticated. I look up at the clock and I smile to myself because everything is going to be perfect.

I had stopped by uninvited one day to see him when I first got back in town for two reasons. The first was to see if anyone else was there with him. The second to scope out the surroundings, to see if any changes were made or anything added that would say a woman now lives here.

After I was sure there was no sign of a woman's possessions, I put my plan into motion.

Trying to get his attention has been difficult because he didn't come to dinner, which surprised me. I even told him Mom and Dad would be looking forward to having him join us. Not to mention he has not been answering any of my calls. That is when today's plan came into fruition. If Goliath won't come to the mountain, then the mountain must go to Goliath. Or something to that effect...

"And for dessert", I say as I fling out a new red lingerie piece that I had ordered from Fredrick's of Hollywood. "Hmm, yeah, I think Evan will definitely be pleasantly surprised," I say to myself as I hold up this little sexy thing. Sexy is an understatement. This laced red floral crotch-less bodysuit with the open side and back will have Evan dropping to his knees and thanking me all night long. The sex between Evan and I have always been good. He knew it and I knew it. Before me, he was happy with just an orgasm; I showed him what it took to please a woman. I taught him all the different ways to make a woman reach an orgasm. He became the best lover I ever had. Traveling around the globe, I still couldn't find anyone that made me feel like Evan. I yearned for his touch. After seeing him the other day, my body started aching for him. That just confirmed that I made the right decision to come home.

Candles lit, table set and that all took less than an hour. I glance down at my Ebel 18kGold diamond encrusted watch and smile. "Perfect" I say with a self-assured smirk. I have just enough time to get in the shower and be ready to get this party started.

Alexia

"Thank you, Art, I'll see you in four weeks," I say as I make a mad dash out of the hair salon. I swear if Art wasn't the best Loc Technician in New York, I would not spend the whole day in that spot. As I drive up 188th Street to the Grand Central Parkway, I cannot help but to think back on how I met Art.

"Excuse me Miss, but would you allow me to play in your hair?"

I swiveled my bar stool around so that I could hear this person better. "Excuse me, I don't think I heard you," I said.

"Hello, my name is Artiest, and I would like to create a masterpiece in your hair," he said as he handed me a business card. As I took the business card and read it, yes it read *Artiest (Art) Stylist – Creating masterpieces one Loc at a time.* Not only was the shop located on Jamaica Avenue in Queens, but it was close to my old neighborhood, so that had me sold. Two years later and the rest was history. I glance in the mirror and pat my new hair style. Yes, Art was right! This back sweep with three French braids is nice and it will keep for the month or a little longer.

As I check the digital clock on the dashboard for the time, I sigh in relief. I still have time to go by my place and pick up a couple of outfits to take back to Evan's. It has been a glorious couple of months with Evan. When I dropped by his house that evening two months ago, I didn't think that everything would have turned out the way it had. With him being on vacation we spent a lot of time together. We made love first thing in the morning, then again in the shower and if I didn't push him away from me, I am sure we would have made love at the front door. In the mornings, we go our separate ways, me going to the café and him to the bakery. We talked on the phone a couple of times throughout the day. We even started sexting, which I personally have grown to like and look forward to.

I could not believe it last night when Evan presented me with a little black box. The velvet box was wrapped in a beautiful red ribbon. Thoughts ran through my head like an Olympic sprinter staring at that box. Yeah, I have been having a good time with Evan. Yeah, he makes me feel things I never felt before, but it has only been … Oh My God! … He can't be asking me to … it is too soon, isn't it? I'm not ready to do this all over again, am I? He hasn't even said the three magical words. Shoot I haven't even said those three magical words, not out loud anyway. He just can't be asking me to, not yet… not now.

"Alexia, would you do me the honor of accepting this gift," he said as he slid the box toward me.

As I came back into focus and reached for the box, I began to undo the ribbon and pry at the box. Evan says, "I leave so early in the morning to go to work. So, the nights that you stay over I want you to be able to sleep as late as you can."

I opened the box and inside was a set of keys. One said *front one* and the other said front *two*. The keys were attached to a keychain that had a miniature bus dangling from the end. Under the keys was a small paper with the words *FAITH* and *TRUTH* written on it. I held up the paper and asked, "What is this?" His reply was that it was the password for the alarm system.

Thinking about last night helps me not to get angry that I am sitting in traffic on the Robert F Kennedy Bridge. My plan was to get out of Queens before rush hour. Unfortunately, there are times like today when the time of day does not matter. There is traffic backed up all day.

Perfect, I find a parking space directly in front of Evan's door. Which, to be honest, I should celebrate because in Harlem in the early evening this is a true rarity. As I enter Evan's apartment, I can't help but smile because tonight I'm going to make it special. On my way over here, I stopped at Fairway supermarket and picked up some items to make dinner. Jumbo shrimp, white wine, and pasta. I also picked up the fixings for a delicious salad.

Oh, man I didn't beat Evan home! There goes my surprise. He must have wanted to surprise me because there are candles lit and food warming in the oven. This is why I am falling in love with this man. He is so thoughtful and considerate.

I go running through the rooms and calling out his name, "Evan, Evan"

As I turn the corner and am about to take the stairs two at a time, I stop dead in my tracks. This woman is standing in my path with her hands on hips and a seductive grin pasted on her face. Let me not forget to mention that she is damn near naked! I couldn't believe this woman is standing at the top of the steps with a *welcome home Daddy* look.

"What the hell? Who the hell are you!" I scream out.

"Who am I? No, I should be asking, who the hell are you!" she says as she sashays down the steps in her *baby come get some* red four-inch pumps.

This is ridiculous! Evan just gave me his key last night. Why would he have another woman in his house already? He knew that I was coming back over tonight. I think he knew. I mean, I don't think we spoke about it, but I thought it was just common sense that I would come back tonight. I have been over here every night for the last two weeks. Oh, hell, not again, this can't be happening again. A thousand different thoughts start running rampant in my head, as I try to compose myself.

When she gets to the bottom of the stairs, she turns around and says nastily, "I will repeat myself, who the hell are you?"

"My name is Alexia; I am a friend of Evan's," I say as pleasant as I can because honestly drama is not what I need in my life now.

As I glance around at the room, I now see everything differently. The burning candles and the place setting for two. This romantic evening was not planned for me. Before she could say anything else, I turn around grab my bag and went racing for the door.

As I reach for the handle the door flies open. "Hey Baby, I was hoping to beat you here," Evan says as he steps into the house. He turns to close the door and that his when I notice that he is holding bags in one hand and hiding something behind his back with the other hand.

"Evan I'm sorry, I should've called first," I say as I reach past him to open the door he has just closed.

Before I walk out the door, I turn to him and look him straight in the eyes and ask "Why, Evan? Why?" Seeing my pain and confusion, he asks, "Alexia, what is wrong?"

"Evan, darling you are finally home."

When I hear that voice, I turn around with a quickness. "What are you doing here?" I yell out at her. Before she has a chance to say anything else, I hear the front door slam shut. I barrel out of the door to try and catch Alexia. "Alexia, Alexia" I say as I do my best to try to catch her. I cannot believe just a few moments ago I was so happy to see her car parked in front of my door. Now I wish she had a parking space a little further away. I reach her just as she closes the door and when she turns to look at me, I truly do not recognize the person staring back at me. The hurt and pain written all over her face makes her unrecognizable to me.

"Alexia please don't leave like this. Please let me talk to you, please don't leave like this."

All my pleading fell on deaf ears because Alexia just pulled off without even looking back.

I run back into the house, and I cannot believe Jazmyne is sitting there half naked sipping on something that I'm sure is champagne.

I'm sure Jazmyne is celebrating the whole scene that unfolded a few seconds ago.

"What are you doing here, and most importantly how did you get into my house? I should call the cops on you for breaking into my house!" I yell at Jazmyne.

All the years we were together, I had never given her a key. The only woman that I was ever moved to give a key to my place was Alexia. I just gave Alexia the keys last night and then this today. As I grab my cell phone to call Alexia, Jazmyne gets up off the sofa and walks into the kitchen. I must be going crazy because I can't believe she is really parading around in my spot with damn near no clothes on. She hasn't said a word since Alexia left.

"What is all this?" I say, trying to make sense of how my world just turned upside down.

She turns around and it is then that I notice what Alexia must have gotten a full view of. That thing looks like it is barely covering her up. Her breasts are tucked in, and you can see her protruding nipples. The same nipples that I spent so many hours sucking and kissing a long time ago. As she bent down to pick up something off the floor, I got a full view of her entry way to heaven (that is what she had me call her vagina). Before I could betray myself and Alexia, I turn around and tell her to get dressed. I will pack up all this stuff she brought over here for her while she changes.

"Evan I'm sorry," she sings as she walks up behind me. "I was trying to surprise you. Since I haven't been able to catch up to you, I figured you were working too hard like always. I remembered where you kept the extra key and I just let myself in. I wanted to have dinner ready for you and then a special dessert just for you."

I could feel Jazmyne behind me, so I turn around to face her.

"You should've called first" and before I could finish what I was saying, her lips were on mine and her tongue was in my mouth.

I push her off me. "What are doing? Have you lost your mind?" I ask her as I pace around my kitchen.

"Evan, you have not returned any of my calls, what else was I supposed to do?"

"For starters, go upstairs and put some clothes on. I cannot talk to you when you are standing here half naked."

When she returns fully clothed, I tell her exactly what is on my mind.

"How dare you just show up at my spot, again. Jazmyne, I am not sure what kind of game you are playing, but I don't want any part of it," I say to her while trying to keep my anger at bay.

"Evan, I am sorry. I remembered where you left the spare key and I thought I would surprise you with dinner," she tries to explain as I notice the tears forming in her eyes.

"You can keep the food; I will just leave. Once again Evan I apologize for not calling first," she says as she walks to the door.

I can't believe I am starting to feel guilty about this whole thing. Like I had done something wrong. I had done nothing wrong. I have finally met a woman that I enjoy being with. One who I look forward to spending more time with. In fact, someone I look forward to spending all my time with. And now it is all in jeopardy.

"Wait, wait don't leave just yet. We need to talk so something like this does not happen again." As I guide her to the living room and gesture for her to take a seat, I begin. "Jazmyne, it has been two years since we spoke. You made it very clear that you were moving on. At first, I was hurt, no… I was devastated. You were the first woman that I loved. You taught me how to love a woman. But I have finally moved on. I did not return any of your calls because I have no interest in seeing or talking to you again."

"I admit I should have handled it like a man and just been honest with you the first night you popped up over here. You have always taken what you wanted. Your sense of entitlement always got in the way of the beautiful person that you are."

She sat there with her legs crossed and that right leg shaking. I could tell she did not like what I was saying. But that was the least of my concern right now.

"You came over unannounced because you wanted to, and the hell with everyone else." Before I could finish, she stood up ran her hands down her skirt to smooth it out, picked up her overnight bag and handbag and said, "Evan, I refuse to sit here and let you talk to me this way. I have already said I was sorry, and I promise you I will not grace your doorstep again."

She then slams the door behind her.

I cannot help but to crack up at the irony of it all. Why did I feel the need to explain anything to her? Was I wrong for trying to set her straight? Something is truly up with her because the Jazmyne that I knew would not have taken so kindly to being told a thing or two. I grasp my head to massage my temple to try and release the stress I am feeling.

I try calling Alexia again but to no avail. I am sure she has now turned her phone off or blocked me because it is going straight to voicemail.

Three Weeks
Later...

I feel so relaxed and at ease as I sit here on the balcony of my beautiful villa in the most beautiful place in the world. Looking out over the beach and witnessing the rising of the sun, I see why my father loved Aruba. He would always brag about how magical of an island it was. Having this timeshare allowed my parents to spend a month on this island that is known as the "Happy Island".

After the incident with Evan, I left New York and arrived in Aruba the very next day. I have been here for three weeks- three *glorious* weeks. I have spent my time sightseeing and on the pristine beaches, relaxing catching up on my reading. My Kindle was filled with books I had downloaded and hadn't had any time to read. I rented a car when I arrived so that I could explore the island on my terms and my own time. During one of my day trips, I decided that this would be a perfect place to open a second café. Yes, Aruba is a tourist hot spot, but the locals would appreciate what *Chocolate, Books & More* has to offer.

The villa that I'm staying at has two awesome pools; one has a waterfall and is located at the quiet end of the resort and the other has a swim up bar and is situated at the opposite end of the resort. This end of the resort seems to be livelier with the guests. When I am not relaxing on the beach, this is where I spend my time. I have made friends with the bartender named George. I was happy to hear that George knew my parents. He told me how this is a very family-oriented resort. They were all very sad to hear of the passing of my parents. George would have my pina colada waiting for me every day during happy hour. Each day we would talk and in one of our conversations, I told him of my thoughts to open a café. He expressed genuine excitement for my idea. He volunteered to help me any way he could.

In one of our chats, George mentioned that his wife was from New York. He said that he would love for me to meet her. He invited me to his home for dinner and I met his beautiful wife, Michelle. Michelle is from Harlem, and she moved to Aruba to live with her father who was Aruban. She has been in Aruba for twenty years and married to George for fifteen of those. She explains how when she left New York and arrived on this beautiful island, Starbucks was just starting to come on the scene. She says they have a local café, but it is nothing like *Chocolate, Books & More* would be. George shared my ideas with her, and she was excited about the new possibilities it would bring to the Island.

After dinner, I use this time to fill them in on all the changes taking place in Harlem and The Bronx. I tell her that she would not recognize Harlem or the Bronx now at all. Before she left, she knew change was inevitable but had hoped Harlem would just keep that Harlem feel. With a glimmer of sadness in her voice she says,

"Harlem was just beginning to gentrify before I relocated, and it was hurting my heart to see the changes."

She shares her memories of growing up in Harlem and her mom and dad going to the Cotton Club or the Lenox Lounge. She talks about that train ride every Saturday morning to visit her grandmother in The Bronx.

After another hour or so we decide to call it a night. They drive me back to my villa and we say our goodnights. I thank them for a beautiful evening. They inform me that I have an open invitation to return. Michelle asks, "How much longer will you be in Aruba." I could not answer her right away because honestly, I did not know. Before getting out of the car, Michelle places in my hand the number to a local realtor, who I promise to call the following day.

Alexia

After having dinner with George and Michelle, Michelle and I have become good friends. We now speak on the phone every day and have had lunch together at least three times. I was finally able to get in contact with Jody, the realtor that Michelle recommended. Today the three of us are meeting for lunch. Jody goes over the details with me about owning a business in Aruba. There are a quite a bit of technicalities that must be worked out and forms that have to be filed. An application for a business license is needed. Michelle suggests I speak with someone at the bank for information on sending money over. Since I am not an Aruban Dutch local, I will need to set up residence in Aruba. Michelle also explains it may be a little easier if I have a local Aruban Dutch citizen go into business with me. Michelle offers herself and George as business partners. Jody then explains to me that I should come back to Aruba and apply for a six-month visa.

All this information is a lot to take in but I'm thinking it will be well worth it. Once we finish going over some of the business aspects, she drives me around Aruba for about three hours. She shows me many different locations that will work for my café. We stop and have lunch at a local spot. The food is good, and the owner is from New Jersey. Michelle, Jody and I go over all the properties that I saw today, and I am able to narrow it down to three possibilities that sparked my interest.

Still thinking about those locations as I walk into the villa, I notice the stack of mail on the counter.

LaJune has been sending me mail on a weekly basis since I came here. I would usually go through and shred all the junk mail. I pay all my bills, personal and business, on-line and having opted into paperless billing, I don't get much mail other than junk mail. What I do notice is a letter from David. As surprising as that is, my next move is more surprising.

I go into the kitchen to get a glass of wine, but on second thought I decide to take the whole bottle of Moscato along with a glass to the living room.

My Dearest Alexia,

I hope this letter finds you well. If you are reading this, then I want to Thank You. I will start off by asking for your forgiveness. I did so many things wrong in my quest of loving you. For I have always loved you.

When you left me, I knew that I had messed up the best thing that had happened and would ever happen to me. You were and still are a strong and independent woman. You did not need me to define your self-worth. This, Alexia, is something I have always known about you. My actions were inexcusable. I am now trying to make amends with you.

When your parents were killed, I wanted to be there for you. I wanted desperately to show you I could be the husband you deserve. I wanted to do something to make up for the pain I caused you throughout our marriage. When you served me with those divorce papers, it was the finality of it all that I could not accept.

I refused to sign the divorce papers for as long as I could. I was holding out hoping you would allow me to show you that I have changed. For me, we were always meant to be together. I love you Alexia and I hope more than anything you know that. I was a fool for the way that I treated you. It was as if the more strength you showed, the less of a man I felt.

Alexia, I have changed. I even started going to church. Yeah, yeah, I know you are shocked. But I found myself needing something and that was the only thing that made sense at the time.

I have become active in the youth group. Being a mentor to a group of young men seems to be my calling. Who would've thought me a big brother? But I am really enjoying this, helping young men. All of this has helped me to see my shortcomings. It has also helped me see that I needed to stop what I was doing to you. I needed to ask you for your forgiveness. I have realized that by not signing the papers, I was being very selfish. I was trying to hold on to the hope of us getting back together. The last few months I have been keeping an eye on what you have been doing. Alexia, I am very proud of you and what you are accomplishing. I have been into your café, and it is all that you wanted. At the time, you brought the idea to me, my reaction was one of a man in fear. Fear that his woman could and would succeed without him.

I have concluded that I must let you go. And in the process, give up any thought or fantasy of us being together. I am sorry it has taken me so long to realize this. I have been trying to have this conversation face to face with you. I am not surprised that you have not taken any of my calls or returned them. I am hoping that you at least read this letter. Writing you was my last option without everything being handled by our lawyers.

So, Alexia I have signed the papers and I pray that you will find it in your heart to forgive me. I sincerely wish that one day we can at least be friends.

May God continue to bless and keep you.

David

I had not realized I was crying until I tasted the salty tears roll down my lips. As I finish the letter, I cry tears of happiness for David.

David was miserable and he needed to move on. A person cannot live like that and have a fulfilled life.

Reading his letter and hearing him talking about changing has me realizing that I needed to do some changing also. I also realize that it would not have hurt me to take one of his many calls.

I need to move on also. I need to let some stuff go. I ran from Evan. I ran all the way to Aruba. That may not have been the smartest thing to do. Evan is not David

"No, Evan is not David!" I scream as I jump up from the chaise I am laying on.

As I run into the bedroom and start throwing my clothes into my suitcase, all I can say is, "I need to get home to my man, my man!" Why did I fly off the handle? "Literally fly," I say as I start cracking myself up at the thought of how I must've looked making a mad dash to the airport to get out of town so quickly.

I start checking flights on my laptop to see what I can book to get back home. I lucked up when I was coming out here. When I arrived at the airport there were a few cancellations, so the ticket agent booked me on the first available flight. Now that I am trying to get back home, finding a last-minute flight is looking almost impossible.

It takes me five days to get all my business together. I call Jody and tell her I was returning to New York, but I had decided on the location of my café. Once we discussed everything, I inform her Michelle would be the person to contact. My next call was to Michelle. I explain everything to her, and she agreed to handle everything for me in Aruba. I will return to Aruba soon, but right now I need to go home.

Evan

It has been a long three weeks. A *very* long three weeks. I have not seen nor heard from Alexia.

All my calls have gone unanswered. Each time I go by the café, I am told she is not in. The two young ladies that work there have started looking at me pitifully when I show up.

I have even written a few letters, which have also gone unanswered.

I have been doing everything to keep my mind off Alexia. I hang out with my boys and stay busy. I even agreed to go away for an all-boys getaway. My man James is getting married next month. This will be his last hurrah before the big day.

"Hey Ellis, you got a minute?" I say as I walk into Ellis' office and flop down in the chair across from his desk.

"What's up, you ready for your getaway?" Ellis asks, chuckling.

"What's so funny?" I respond, not really amused.

"Nothing man, I'm just thinking about you guys all together and all the trouble you all will be getting yourselves into."

"I need to make sure I have some bail money put aside. I know James is going to act like a straight up fool," Ellis says, while cracking himself up.

"Alright, alright with the jokes already," I say, not in the mood.

"Listen, I'm sorry but I remember how you boys used to be. Trouble was not too far behind when you all hung out. I may not have been around much because I was doing my own thing, but I would see you all trying to be bad. I'm just glad that each of you had a good head on your shoulders and was just going through a phase," Ellis says changing his tone a bit to reflect my mood.

"You know James has changed since he got with Sharon. I would have thought we would be going somewhere like Vegas but no we going to Aruba," I say as I do my best to keep myself from laughing.

This feels so good clowning and talking to my brother and not thinking about Alexia. Well, I wasn't thinking about Alexia, until just now. It is funny how she seems to creep into my thoughts. I cannot believe that she has not returned any of my calls or messages. I know the incident was jacked up with Jazmyne, but no communication for three weeks. Now that is some straight up bull.

"Evan, Earth to Evan come in," I can hear Ellis saying as he is snapping his fingers. It is as if when Alexia comes to mind, she blocks out everything and everyone else.

"Yeah, yeah I hear you," I say as I get up and walk to the other side of the room.

"Have you heard anything from Alexia?" he asks.

"Nope, still no word, I cannot believe that she has not tried to contact me yet. What I'm not understanding is, I honestly thought we shared something special."

"Didn't you say that she walked in on Jazmyne damn near naked in your kitchen?" Ellis says nudging my memory of that crazy day.

"I remember the details, thank you brother," I say as I shake my head. "The short time we spent together we talked about everything but our past relationships. I knew she was married and hurt by her soon to be her ex-husband, but we never discussed the details. And I never shared the details of Jazmyne because Jazmyne is the last person I was thinking about while I was with Alexia." Saying that out loud sounds very stupid. But if I am going to be honest, I must say we were spending all our time trying to get to know each other. The things we talked about had absolutely nothing to do with others who were part of our past.

As I try explaining everything to my brother, it becomes very clear that just maybe we were rushing it. I had just given her a key to my house. I have never given anyone a key to my place. Being with Alexia did something to me. She was the first thing I thought of in the morning and the last thing I thought of at night. During the day, my thoughts were consumed with her. The nights that she stayed over at my place, I swear I've never slept so peaceful. I looked forward to pleasing her. I found out that she likes taking long bubble baths while listening to Al Jarreau. So, I took great pleasure in having a bubble bath waiting for her. I would have scented candles and Al Jarreau playing on the sound system. Pleasing her had become my personal mission and brought me great pleasure as well.

Ellis is trying to convince me that all is not lost. He is telling me to just be patient and give her time.

I share with him that Alexia has stolen my heart and I will give her all the time she needs to come back to me.

"So, getting back to Aruba," Ellis says, "and if I may ask, how did you party animals come up with a bachelor party in Aruba?" he says snickering.

"Don't ask brother, please don't ask," I say while shaking my head. "My plan is to make this the best bachelor party for my man. There will be a lot of beer and liquor on deck. Brother let me get out of here so I can hash out all the last-minute details that I need to work out before we take off," I say to Ellis as I make my exit out of the office.

"I have some bail money put aside, just in case," Ellis hollers at my back while he is cracking up.

Lajune

Alexia has been gone for three weeks. I am not sure I agree with the way my girl high tailed it out of here, but one thing is for certain, it doesn't matter whether I agree or not, I got her back. Before she left, she asked me to look in on the girls at the café. Those two girls are heaven sent for real. I only had to go by and pick up the daily deposits; besides that, they had everything running smoothly. When there is a problem, they do not hesitate to call me and call me is what they did when Evan was constantly showing up. Not that he was becoming a problem, but I think they were just starting to feel uncomfortable.

Alexia did not leave any instructions on how to deal with Evan, but I just knew not to tell him where she had run off to. I assumed when she was ready to deal with him, she would. I have been going by her place to collect the mail and water her plants. At the end of each week, I would put all the mail in a large manila envelope and forward it to her. I truly was feeling sorry for Evan because in the beginning there was a letter from him every day.

The last batch of mail I sent even had a letter from David. Now that one, I started to trash and not even send but, even I know, that would've been dead wrong. Plus, it was not my place. So, I just sent it and prayed that fool didn't cause my girl any more stress.

With everything that was going on with Alexia, I was starting to feel a little worn down. Since my girl wasn't here, I haven't been out to eat and there are days that I don't eat at all. I have even allowed my walking to fall off. This morning, as I was getting ready for work, I had to change outfits three times. Nothing was fitting right. Honestly nothing has been fitting right for a minute now, but I have gotten very good at layering, so no one can tell.

I did notice that I had to add an extra layer of concealer under my eyes. It seems as if the dark circles are getting darker. For a person who does not wear a lot of makeup, I was really starting to feel uncomfortable with all this gook on my face. I had no choice though after one of my clients noticed a change in my appearance and asked if everything was ok. She said my face had a sunken-in look. She then patted my hand and said, "It's ok dear, we all go through something." She then gave me a list of makeup products she used to help freshen up her impeccable look. They were expensive but they did the trick. For some reason, this morning nothing seems to be working.

Finally, out of the house and thanking God for late mornings. My first client meeting is at 10:00 this morning. This would normally be late for me, but the client that I am meeting with starts work at 6:00 in the mornings and she only works for a couple of hours each day. I was lucky to be able to get an appointment with her at all. So yes, this 10:00 am is perfect for me.

Since I live on 116th Street, I decide to take the train. I hate taking cabs. The driver usually has a horrible body odor, and the inside of the cab usually smells awful. I run down the stairs of the station because I can hear the roaring of the train as it is approaching my station.

Of course, the train is packed, and I can't find a seat. I start feeling funny. My head starts spinning and I realize in that moment that I need to start exercising again because that little jog down the steps got me feeling all kinds of woozy.

I must've looked crazy because this lady was offering me her seat. Just as I thanked her and was about to take the seat, my head felt as if someone had hit me with a hammer. Everything around me got dark and fuzzy. The last thing I remember hearing is someone asking, "Miss, Miss are you ok?"

hat do they call it … "fate"? The development of events beyond a person's control, regarded as determined by a supernatural power. Yeah, it had to be fate.

I had arrived at the airport early. Had enough time to sit in the lounge and get some breakfast. I decided to give Evan a call and let him know that I was on my way home. Getting his voicemail, I left a simple message "Sorry and I Love you." Was that too much? Or was it too little? I don't know but I just wanted to say those four simple words now and would handle the rest later.

I tried calling LaJune again. I have not been able to get in contact with my girl in a minute and I'm starting to get worried. Even if we don't see each other for weeks, we would still reach out through text or email just to keep the communication lines open. We both have come to depend on these small pieces of our sisterhood. The smiley face good morning or the small waving of the hand emoji, which we understood to mean *I am waving at you from way over here.*

I miss the martini glass emoji, which she adds to the end of her text to let me know she was in desperate need of a martini.

She must be having a very hectic time at work, is what I am thinking as I shut down my laptop and try to take a quick nap. Just as I was about to enter dream land, I hear an announcement coming over the PA system. "Attention passengers, Flight number 1765 to New York John F Kennedy Airport will now be leaving from gate 6."

Realizing that is my flight, I murmur "great" as I begin to gather my belongs. Once I exit the lounge, I start looking for signs that would lead me to the correct gate area. Just my luck Gate 6 is all the way on the other side of the terminal. Looking at my watch, I send up a silent prayer that I am early. I still have two hours before my boarding process begins. I hate that they make these airports so large now. Aruba International is not as big as my two hometown airports, JFK and LaGuardia, but it is big, nonetheless.

As I make my way through the airport, I cannot help but to think of Evan and all the explaining I will be doing. Once I made up my mind to return home and to my man, I read all the letters LaJune had forwarded to me. I also listened to all the voice mails and read all the text massages Evan left. He apologized profusely about the incident with what's her name. I cannot bring myself to say her name. He took a lot of time to explain his side of the story, which all makes sense to me now. If I had only taken the time to listen to him before, we would not be in this situation now. That I am sure of. Once I finally find the gate for my flight, I collapse into a seat in the waiting area. As I look out the window at the planes arriving and departing, my mind starts drifting back to the first time I met Evan and eventually I fall asleep. I wake up right as my flight begins to board. My flight is thankfully uneventful, and I am even able to get another quick nap. I must be more exhausted than I thought because even with the nap at the airport and the nap on the plane, my body still doesn't feel recharged as the seatbelt light turns off and passengers start retrieving their bags from the overhead compartments. I am one of the last passengers off the plane because I decide to let the rush of passengers get off before even moving from my seat.

As I get close to the exit to get a taxi, I am still thinking about Evan and practicing what I will say to him when we finally speak

In his voice mails, he shared how he has never felt this way for anyone before. He said that he would be heartbroken if he never had the opportunity to love me the way I deserve to be loved. He explained that maybe we were moving too fast. He would be willing to slow down to a pace that is suitable and maybe more comfortable for me.

"Dang, I love that man," I say into the air to no one in particular. I must've not been paying attention to where I was going because just then I collide with a man.

"I'm sorry," I say as we look at each other and then down to all my papers on the floor.

"No, no, I'm sorry. I was not looking where I was going." After a slight pause, he then says, "Let me help you pick up your stuff."

This gorgeous man is trying to explain to me how he bumped into me when in fact I wasn't paying attention to where I was going, and I know I bumped into him.

As we both kneel to gather up my things that have scattered across the floor, I hear a voice. That voice, it sounds so familiar, but I am sure it can't be who I think it is.

"Come on man, we ain't even get on the flight yet and already you…" He suddenly stops what he was saying as if the words got caught in his throat.

At the same time, I look up and everything that I just picked up from the floor goes flying back down.

"Evan," I whisper.

Evan

My boys and I are all set for the bachelor party getaway. I would have preferred going to Las Vegas for some fun filled couple of days. Sharon, James's fiancé suggested that we go to Aruba since James owns a timeshare there. Not wanting to create any grief between my man and his lady, I agreed. Aruba it is. But what they don't know is that I made a reservation at a different hotel. My coworker hooked me up with his timeshare, so I went with his. Plus, this hotel is on the opposite side of the Island. I really didn't like the idea of Sharon having access to where we were going to be staying. This is supposed to be my homie's last weekend as a single man with the fellas. I had pre-arranged the fridge and bar to be stocked with all our favorites. This way the party will start as soon as we check-in.

I look out the window as we arrive at JFK and my thoughts quickly go to Alexia. It has been over a month and still no word. I have done everything I know to do. Everything I have tried has been to no avail. So now I am leaving it up to God and Alexia. When she is ready to contact me, she will. I just pray that God helps her get ready soon because I miss her terribly.

We get our bags from the trunk of the taxi and go inside the airport to begin the check in process. My gift to everyone was an upgrade to first class. With the first-class seats, we will be the first ones on and off the plane. I already have the car service scheduled to pick us up once we arrive in Aruba. I'm excited to see the looks on their faces with the upgrades. Kev is in the middle of one of his dramatic stories. He is enlightening us about his latest date. The young lady he went out with last night was related to the chick he dated a few months back. He said he felt like he had met her before but wasn't sure. The young lady then told him where and how she met him. He said he couldn't get her home quick enough. He said she wanted him to go upstairs for a night cap. He remembered how crazy her cousin was and as tempted as he might have been for a night cap, he had to refuse. We all couldn't help but crack up laughing because only Kev could get himself in such a crazy situation. James turns around to tell Kev something and just then he collides with a woman walking in his direction.

That beautiful woman that had all her papers knocked out of her hand is Alexia. I cannot believe it. My heart stops and what I was about to say to James gets stuck in my throat.

Standing a few feet in front of me is the woman that has changed my life. "Alexia what are you doing here?" I finally ask as my thoughts and voice are starting to come back to me.

Seeing Evan at the airport has me in complete shock. Even though I was praying to see him once I got home, this catches me off guard. Once we each gather our thoughts, he explains he is going to Aruba for his friends' bachelor party. With my heart beating a mile a minute and my mouth moving just as fast, I try telling him that Aruba is where I have been since the incident at his house.

I didn't think the time was right but the here and now is all we have. I begin to apologize for leaving the way I did. I explain to Evan my feelings and then my actions. I glanced over at his friends and noticed they were starting to look impatient. "Evan when will you be back in the city? Before he could answer I had to throw in, "I really would like to talk to you and honestly this is not the time or place."

"You're right Alexia, and I agree about the timing. We have to catch our flight," he says glancing back at his boys

"Please, can I stop by to see you when I get back to New York Sunday night?" Evan asks

"Yes Evan, I will be waiting for you," I reply.

He grabs me in an embrace that sweeps me off my feet. He holds me tight. He then takes my face in his hands and places the most passionate kiss on my lips. His kiss is filled with all the love I know he has for me. He kisses me as if I am his lifeline. As if his mere existence becomes complete with me. I return his kiss as if my life depends on him, because in fact it does. This moment, this embrace, this kiss is exactly what I need. I know right then that Evan loves me. The hardest thing for me to do is to let him go. It took everything within me to step out of that embrace. Well, it did help when I remember we are in the middle of the airport. Also, his buddies are on the sideline screaming "Get a room why don't cha!"

"Your buddies are waiting for you, You, need to go," I say as I start to reluctantly push him toward them.

He looks over at them and chuckles. He kisses me quickly and then jogs over to where the gang is waiting. "I'll call you," he says over his shoulder and blows me a kiss.

Alexia

After waiting on line for a taxi, I finally get one. Getting a taxi at the airport in New York is way too complicated. I sit in my seat, fasten my seat belt, and rest my head back. At this moment, I am feeling very grateful for the way the day played out.

I close my eyes and thank God for fate.

My first stop is to go by and see my girl LaJune. I must fill her in on everything. I tried calling her a few times from the plane and the taxi, but I couldn't reach her. I know when she is knee deep in work, she doesn't like any interruptions or distractions, but I am positive she wouldn't mind this one.

As my taxi driver pulls up to her brownstone, I sense that something isn't right. Before I can even get out of the car her neighbor Billy greets me with his typical cheery self, "Good morning, Miss

Alexia. How are you doing?" Before I have a chance to respond he tells me, "Miss LaJune hasn't been home in a couple of days. If she was going out of town, she didn't give me the heads up and that's not like her." I stop suddenly on my way up the steps and whip around so I can get a better look at him as if that would help me to get a better understanding of what he just said.

"What do you mean she hasn't been home in a couple of days?" I ask, concern spread all over my face.

He explains how the last time he saw her was when she left to go to work one morning, and she has not been back.

I let myself in her apartment with the set of keys she gave me a while ago, and after looking around I realize Billy is right, she has not been home in a couple of days. Her bedroom was in disarray with clothes thrown all over the place. In the kitchen, there is a half-empty cup of coffee on the counter. LaJune often leaves her coffee cup on the counter when she leaves for work in a hurry. The milk in the coffee has started to curdle and that is evidence it has been on the counter for a couple days.

I flop down on the sofa in the living room and try to put the pieces together. I dig in my bag for my phone so I can call the first place that comes to mind. My mind is spinning in all different directions. Many scenarios start playing in my head. I'm so distracted that I didn't even hear the person on the other end of the phone saying hello.

"I'm sorry. Diana, this is Alexia. Is LaJune in the office?"

"I'm sorry Alexia, LaJune made me promise not to call you. She has been in Columbia Presbyterian Hospital since Monday," Diana informs me.

"What! Since Monday?" I scream in the phone. Diane what happened?" I could not have been possibly so consumed with my life that I did not know my girlfriend was in trouble. I need to get to the hospital right now; everything else will have to wait.

I rush out her brownstone and Billy assists me with a taxi. He must have seen the concern on my face because as he is holding the passenger side door, he asks "Is everything ok, with Miss LaJune?"

My only reply is that I will contact him when I have more details.

As I sit in the taxi, I think back on the conversation with Diana.

"The only information we have is that she passed out on the train on her way in to work. I have been down to see her, but she wasn't taking any visitors". I heard the sadness in Diane voice as she explains everything to me.

"Alexia I would go every day after work to see her. It didn't matter that she didn't want to see anyone. I just wanted her to know I was there for her. She has been calling into the office every day to let me know she is doing ok. She made me promise not to call you."

When I arrive at the hospital I go to the visitor's station and ask for LaJune Duncan's room. I am told she is not accepting visitors at this time. I explained that I am her sister and just returned from out of town. It is no one's business that we aren't blood sisters. LaJune is my sister through love. The receptionist apologizes and informs me that I can go to the 9th floor, which is the visitor's waiting area. Once I get on that floor, I can request to speak with her doctor or nurse.

I have to wait a few minutes while they page her doctor. I did not realize the time or how long it has been since my plane landed in New York, until my cell phone starts vibrating.

"Hello Alexia, it's Evan. Did you make it home ok?"

"Evan, it's LaJune," is all I can say before the tears and all the emotions that I have been holding in comes out.

After explaining everything to him and telling him about her not wanting any visitors, I tell him where I am and how I am waiting for a doctor or nurse to come and speak with me.

Evan says he wishes he could be here with me. He makes me promise to call him as soon as I hear something. After ending the call, I look around the visitor's waiting area and notice how warm and comfortable it is. There are televisions on the wall as well as a coffee and tea station. They even have snacks, fruit, water, and juice on the counter for anyone to enjoy.

Just then I hear my name being called. The doctor introduces himself as Dr. Jeff. Once the introductions are over, he asks me if I have any idea as to what is going on with my sister. I respond that I do not have any idea.

He went on to explain that she is suffering from bulimia nervosa or commonly known as bulimia.

The look that I give him must show my confusion, so he continues by explaining that it is an eating disorder where LaJune would binge eat and then self-inflict vomiting to bring up what she just ate.

This was all a little too much for me to understand. He could not be talking about my friend.

"Dr. Jeff are you sure you are talking about LaJune Duncan?" I ask.

"Alexia, I know this is a lot to absorb right now, but I need you to be prepared for what you see when you see her. You are going to see LaJune in her true state not what she has been letting you to see."

I threw up my hands to stop him from talking. I am not understanding what he is talking about. "Dr. please, what are you saying?" I say as I shake my head in disbelief.

I feel a hand on my shoulder. When I turn around, I could

have sworn I was looking into Evan's eyes, but Evan was miles away in Aruba.

"Alexia, I'm Ellis. Evan called me and asked me to come be with you."

Once again, the water works come down. I could not speak any words, but manage to whisper, "thank you".

Ellis went on to introduce himself to Dr. Jeff.

Dr. Jeff continues to tell us about LaJune's current state. He explains she has lost a significant amount of weight and her skin is very pale and blotchy. He explains she has been hospitalized for almost a week and she looks much better now than when she first came in. He tells us she is under psychiatric care as well. Once he finishes, he asks me if I have any questions for him.

"When can I see her?" is the only thing I want to know.

"I am going in to see her now. I will tell her that you are here. This is a very delicate situation, Alexia. I will let her know I have talked with you and explained everything. If she is comfortable with you seeing her, I will call down to the receptionist and have it cleared for you to come up" After that he gives me his card and says goodbye.

Ellis takes my hand. "Alexia, I wish we would've met under better circumstances. But Evan called me in such a state. He told me where you were and told me to get over here. He didn't want you to be alone. How are you holding up? Is there anything I can do?" he asks.

"Ellis, thank you so much. I just can't seem to grasp everything that is going on."

"I returned from Aruba with so much happiness and joy. I was literally floating on cloud nine. My first instinct was to run to LaJune and fill her in on everything." Once again, the water works start and this time it feels as if they aren't going to stop.

I fill Ellis in on everything that transpired to get me here. I also fill him in on what the doctor said before he got here.

I finally hear my name being paged to come to the receptionist area. I am so relieved.

I am going in to see LaJune. Ellis asks if I would like him to go with me. I assure him that I will be fine. He said that he will take this time to call Evan and give him an update.

Walking into LaJune's room, I see a shell of my best friend. I mean I was only gone for a month. "Boo-bay" I cry as I go to her and hug and cradle her in my arms.

"I'm sorry," she cries.

"No, no, no you have nothing to be sorry about, I should have been paying more attention," I say, the tears now streaming uncontrollably.

She then laughs and I see a glimpse of my girl peek out under all that darkness.

"What is so funny?" I ask while wiping tears from my face.

"You are," she says. "I knew you would not accept me not taking visitors, and when they said your sister is here, I knew it was you."

"Did you really expect me to just leave like ok I'll come back," I say as I take a quick look around the room. There were so many tubes going into her.

"Don't be frightened by all of this," she says as she waves her arm around. "I'm getting better. I will be getting out of here soon," she explains to me.

"That's good," I say, feeling the tears welling back up.

We talk about a little bit of everything and really nothing. I am not sure if I should ask questions or just continue following her lead. After about forty minutes, the nurse comes in with medication and I take that as my cue to leave.

After telling her that I will see her tomorrow and kissing her on the cheek, I leave the room. I get back to the ninth floor and Ellis is there waiting for me. I collapse in his arms.

Once I get myself together, we walk over to BBQ's to get something to eat and to talk.

I tell him that the person I saw today was not my best friend, my Boo-Bay LaJune

"Your what?" he asks with a quizzical look.

"Oh, I'm sorry, 'my Boo-Bay', is what I call her"

"She is my ride or die chick. She always holds me down, no matter what"

"We haven't even known each other that long but it feels like I have known her all my life. My boo. My baby. My sister, my friend," I explain as I choke back tears.

Just thinking about my girl has my emotions all messed up.

"Gotcha," Ellis says.

As I am talking with Ellis, things start to add up. Like all the times she would go to the bathroom after we would eat. The mints, the wearing too much makeup. OMG, those were all signs, and I was too absorbed in my own life that I didn't pay any attention to my best friend's pain.

Ellis takes my hand and does his best to assure me that none of this is my fault. He reminds me that LaJune did a very good job of showing me what she wanted me to see.

A Month Later

As I look out the window at the magnificent garden that this dressing room sits above, I am in awe of God's blessings over my life. I can't believe we are finally here. It has been a month since we both returned from Aruba. LaJune is coming along great. She was moved to an eating disorder hospital in Westchester. She has been there for the last two weeks. She is starting to look like her old self again. Well, better than she did, at least. She had started wearing too much make up and it didn't look right on her. Now I know why, so yeah, she is looking better.

When Evan returned, we talked about everything in our past that had to do with us moving on. I told him about David and the letter that I received from him, which led to me returning home.

Our relationship was a whirlwind. Some say love doesn't happen that fast. Or say it cannot possibly be real if it happens so fast. It has now been less than a year since that first day Evan walked into the café. My life has been forever changed from that first encounter. I am a true believer of love at first sight now.

We both agree that our meeting in the airport was nothing but fate.

Red, yellow, and white roses make a trail to the big white wooden door. I glance down and admire the creativity of my soon to be husband. I cannot help but be amazed at the roses. Red, for the endless love we share. Yellow, for our friendship, which is strong. Finally white, for the purity and sincerity of our commitment to each other.

Who, but my darling Evan would have thought to make a path of roses from my room to the door which I will enter to begin our life together? God truly blessed me when he brought him into my life. This is what is going through my mind as I reach for the gold-plated doorknob.

"No, Alexia let me get it," Ellis says as he places his hand over mine.

"Alexia, you look very beautiful. Evan is a very lucky man to be marrying someone as beautiful as you. I am very glad my brother met you. I am sure you will make him very happy. Our parents would have loved you, Alexia. They both would be telling you what I am about to say. Welcome to the family Alexia and I hope we are a blessing to you as you are to us."

"Thank you, Ellis," I whisper in his ear as he pulls me into a very tender brotherly hug.

My heart is overwhelmed by the love and support that I feel right now for this family. I was so happy when Ellis agreed to walk me down the aisle and give me away as my father would have done had he been alive.

As I walk down the aisle toward my future, I cannot believe I am doing this marriage thing again. I feel in my heart that this time is right. I deserve this. I deserve him. Looking down at Evan, my heart beats a little quicker and my steps speed up a little. I wish I could run down the aisle to this man.

I look over at the faces that are staring back at me, and I cannot help but to feel blessed and highly favored.

I cannot believe this gorgeous woman is walking down the aisle to me. An angel is what she is and today she seems to be just gliding across the floor. She is as elegant as she is beautiful, and she has agreed to be my wife. I cannot help to think that I finally got this right. This love thing has proven to be all that I hoped it would be. When I look up and see Alexia coming down the aisle toward me, it is as if she is walking to the rhythm of my beating heart. I deserve this. I deserve her. Our eyes meet and the glow that I see in her eyes lets me know that our hearts are beating together to the music that only we hear.

The End (for now)

**Stay tuned for Book 2 in the *I Deserve* series titled:
I Desire (Ellis & LaJune's story)**

Book Club Discussion Questions

1. Do you agree that Alexia & Evan's relationship was moving too fast? Why or why not?

2. Did Alexia overreact when she found Jazmyne in Evan's apartment?

3. As LaJune's best friend, should Alexia have picked up on the signs that something was wrong?

4. Did you believe David when he said he wanted Alexia to be happy? Why or why not?

5. Evan and Alexia both lost their parents; do you think this had any bearing on their relationship?

Connect with the author:

Alicia J Evans

Website: aliciajevans.com

Email: aliciajevans@myyahoo.com

Facebook: Alicia Evans

Instagram: @Spin_A__Tale2Tell

Twitter: @LuvlyLocks